THE JU[

A DI REDDING NOVEL

WRITTEN BY
ANDREW HAWTHORNE

Edited by Christopher Watt.

Copyright © 2024 by Andrew Hawthorne

The right of Andrew Hawthorne to be identified as the author of this work has been asserted in accordance with the Copyright, Design and Patents Act 1988.

All rights reserved. This book or any portion thereof may not be reproduced or used in any manner whatsoever without the express written permission of the author and publisher of this work.

Cover photograph and design by

Andrew Hawthorne

Chapter 1

Claire's heart was racing. She was running as hard and as fast as she could. Her breathing was heavy and laboured as she gulped air into her oxygen-starved lungs. Suddenly, she reached the opening and stopped. P&SMAC! Then came the shove. She stumbled onto the road, crossed the nearside lane onto the other lane, only to be hit by the oncoming car.

She screamed out into the night, causing Peter to jump with fright, suddenly awake from his deep sleep. She sat up, now fully awake. She was covered in sweat, her breathing erratic as she tried to calm herself down.

Peter looked up at Claire and gently touched her shoulder. "Was it *the* dream again?" he asked knowingly.

"Yes, I'll be fine. Go back to sleep," she whispered and removed his hand from her shoulder. But she was not fine – she was far from fine. She was as far from fine as she could ever be. Haunted by the memory of the accident, haunted by the loss of their child and most of all, haunted by the loss of trust in the man lying next to her.

Claire had spent six weeks recovering from the accident and the subsequent operation before she had been deemed physically fit. However, this part of her recovery had been quickly followed by four weeks of counselling as she had also been diagnosed with depression. This was to be expected, given her circumstances, but Claire, being Claire, had refused the medication on offer. However, for her to be allowed to return to work, she had agreed to accept the cognitive therapy treatment which her employer had insisted she needed. It had most certainly helped her to cope with the loss of her child; on occasion, she had just sat there with the therapist and cried, which was exactly what she had needed. Eventually, she convinced the therapist that she was on the mend. Of course, she had lied about the dreams and hadn't even mentioned her feelings towards

Peter, otherwise she would never have been given the go-ahead to return to work. That was two weeks ago, and although Claire had returned to work she had since been confined to desk duties—she was completely and utterly bored out of her mind. She had used her time behind the desk to try and find out more information about P&SMAC Holdings Ltd. but had hit a brick wall. Was Peter the person behind the company that paid to have Petrie killed, as she suspected? According to the Swiss bank where the transaction had been made, the account had been closed, and all remaining monies transferred to another account under a new name which they had steadfastly refused to reveal. This was nothing new when dealing with Swiss banks; even Interpol had little influence over them. She had contacted Detective Superintendent Mulholland to see if he had found out any more information but she did not mention her suspicions of Peter's involvement. She couldn't, not without any evidence to back up her theory. Mulholland, who was delighted to hear that Claire was back to work, reminded her that there was still a place for her in the Organised Crime Team if she wanted it. But she couldn't think about that right now. No, she had to find out if Peter was involved in Petrie's death. If he was, the marriage was over. If not, then the marriage might have a chance of surviving this ordeal.

She still loved him. She knew that would never change, but she couldn't live with a killer—even if he didn't commit the act himself. To order and pay for the death of another human being was unacceptable to Claire even if he had done it to protect his family. And so, she could not in all conscience live with him knowing that he was guilty. But she didn't know this for sure and it was torturing her. She also knew that she couldn't confront him without any evidence as that act alone could ruin any chance the marriage had of surviving. Consequently, her life was in complete turmoil. She had to know the truth!

Peter lay there, pretending to sleep. Peter was also a mess but unlike Claire, he had refused counselling. His notion of a perfect life with a family had been completely shattered. Telling Claire that she had lost the baby and then that she couldn't have any more children was the hardest thing he'd ever had to do. It broke him. He had been surprised by Claire's response, or lack thereof, when he had told her about the hysterectomy and didn't know what to do to help her. It was as if she was numb, immune to any further pain and didn't want to acknowledge it, never mind accept it. The shock of losing their unborn child had been traumatic enough and Peter honestly believed that he would never get over it. And, although he was genuinely worried about Claire, who was clearly suffering from depression, he was angry and it was tearing him apart. However, he was also desperate for revenge and someone needed to pay for ruining his chances of having a family. It was all that he cared about.

Despite promises to find out all who had been involved in Claire's assassination attempt, DCI Morrison had come up blank. She had confided in Peter that they suspected his lawyer was involved but they could not prove anything. And so, Peter had decided that he had to do something. Whoever had been involved would pay, one way or the other. He would not rest until justice had been served.

Chapter 2

Breakfast had been a quiet affair which had become the new norm for the MacDonald household. Both Claire and Peter were tired due to the lack of sleep and neither made much of an effort to speak to each other. Sally, their Cocker Spaniel, was as lively as ever and scurried about the kitchen following whoever appeared to be carrying food. After being fed, Sally settled down and lay down in her bed near the backdoor.

Claire left the mid-terraced house in Silverton Avenue at 7.50 a.m., which would give her plenty of time to walk up to Police HQ at Overtoun in time to start her shift at 8.00 a.m. She enjoyed the walk and hoped that the morning air would wake her up. She also hoped that she might be given some more interesting cases to work on. So far, everything DCI Morrison had passed her way had been mundane and she wondered if she had made a mistake not moving to the Organised Crime Team.

She reached the building just before her shift started and made her way upstairs to the CID Corridor where DS Brian O'Neill, DC Jim Armstrong and DC Paul Black were already sitting at their desks. "Morning," she said as she entered the room, taking off her jacket and hanging it on the back of her chair.

"Morning, boss," they all responded.

She walked over to Brian. "Anything exciting to report?"

"Nope. It seems like the night shift had a quiet night."

"Great," said Claire sarcastically, and sat down at her desk, which was face-on to Brian's desk. She opened her laptop and started to sign in. After a few minutes, she was connected to the network and accessed her emails. She quickly scrolled through them. Detective Inspector Michael Butler, who was the duty DI working the night shift, had sent a brief update on the night's highlights and Claire could see that Brian's assessment had been spot on. It had been a quiet night.

"Morning Claire," said DCI Morrison as she entered the room, ignoring the other members of the team.

"Morning, Ma'am," Claire replied automatically.

"I've just received a missing person report and I want you and Brian to investigate."

"A missing person? That's a job for uniform, so…"

"Yes, but this missing person just happens to be a Member of the Scottish Parliament, so the Divisional Commander has requested that we treat it very seriously. Are you up for it? I mean, are you ready to get back out there?"

"Yes, of course," said Claire, delighted that she was finally being allowed to leave her desk. "Who is it?"

"Michael Donaldson, MSP. He's a senior member of the Scottish Government so you will need to be careful. His wife called it in this morning. They live in one of the big houses up the back of Helensburgh. Apparently, she woke up this morning and noticed he hadn't gone to bed last night and seems to have disappeared."

"Abduction?" asked Claire.

"Could be. He's a high-profile politician, but let's not jump to any conclusions. Go, speak to his wife and get the full background. I'll send you the address and the notes from the 999 call. In the meantime, I'll put out an alert to all officers to look out for him. Hopefully, he's just gone off somewhere without telling his wife and will turn up full of apologies."

"Let's hope so," Claire responded. "Come on Brian, grab your jacket. We're off to Helensburgh."

Chapter 3

Claire checked her phone and read out the address to Brian, who nodded in recognition of the street name.

"Yes, that's not far from Hill House. I'll go via the Black Hill," said Brian.

"Hill House? What's that?" asked Claire.

"Have you heard of Charles Rennie Mackintosh?"

"Of course, I have. I'm not completely daft," she said indignantly.

Brian smiled to himself. He loved getting one over on Claire. She might have the university education, but his local knowledge often put her to shame. "Well, he designed the building and a lot of the furniture to go with it. Built in the early 1900s... I think. It's managed by the National Trust or something like that and well worth a visit if you're into that sort of thing. Agnes and I went to see it a few years back."

Claire nodded. "And how is Agnes? Is she coping with the chemotherapy?"

Brian's face changed and he took in a deep breath before speaking. "Yeah, but it's not been easy. It was alright to start with—you know, the first few weeks, but lately she's been suffering a bit with sickness and diarrhoea. They've given her some medication to help but it's not doing a lot of good. She only has another couple of weeks to go though and hopefully that'll be enough treatment to get rid of the cancer."

"Let's hope so," said Claire. "What about the operation? Can't be easy for a woman to lose both breasts."

Brian nodded. "The doctor says that she's recovered really quickly—no infections in the wounds, but she's still a bit sensitive."

"Poor Agnes. Tell her I'm asking for her, will you? I know she's probably not in the mood for visitors right now but when the chemo is finished and she's feeling better, I'd love to see her again."

"She'd like that," said Brian. "And how are you doing? You seem to be a bit brighter now that you're out of the office."

"I'm fine," she lied. "I think this is exactly what I needed."

Brian had been wanting to have this conversation ever since Claire had returned to work but her mood was such that he didn't want to go there. "We're really sorry Claire," he said. He saw the confusion on her face and quickly clarified what he meant. "I mean, Agnes and I are really sorry about... the baby and everything. And that we've not been able to be there for you and Peter."

It took all Claire's strength to hold back the tears which were desperately trying to escape her eyes. "Don't be daft, Brian. You've had enough to contend with, but thanks. It means a lot."

A familiar pinging sound came from Claire's jacket indicating that she had just received a text. She found her phone and read the message.

"The DCI?" asked Brian.

"No, it's from Charlene Tannock, you know, the profiler from Glasgow University."

"Oh, aye. What does she want?"

Claire smiled. "To meet me for a coffee."

~

Peter was working from home that morning. Ever since the COVID pandemic had ended, his work had moved to hybrid working, which meant he could work from home for up to three days per week, if he wanted. He still had to go into the office for team meetings and training, but the new arrangement suited him. He had set up a makeshift office in the small bedroom upstairs. It was perfect for his needs and saved him a great deal of travel time and expense, so it was a win-win as far as he was concerned. However, another key advantage of working from the privacy of his own home was that he could take care of other business without being overheard by a nosy workmate.

He logged on to the PC he used to monitor the markets and then signed into his work laptop and started wading through the emails. Some were from existing clients seeking updates on their investments, others were enquiries from potential new clients with whom he had made initial contact and was keen to woo. In addition to making investments, he was expected to bring in several new customers every year—this was how he was evaluated and assessed by his manager. Failure to reach an agreed target would impact his bonus which made up 50% of his pay. Not that he needed the money—he had made a considerable sum from his own illicit private stockbroker's business, P&SMAC Holdings Limited.

He had terminated the business shortly after he met Claire, but the monies held in secure non-UK bank accounts had been useful to make any payments that he wanted to hide from the authorities. However, soon after paying for the assassination of Petrie, Peter had closed the account and moved the money to another account with a false identity that couldn't be traced back to him. It was incredibly easy to get a false ID in the UK. All you had to do was find someone of similar age who had died, request a copy of their birth certificate from the registration service, rent a property in the name of the deceased, use that address and the birth certificate and a current photo of yourself to apply for a passport and hey presto: a brand-new passport would be delivered to the false address. The only flaw in the process would be if the Passport Office bothered to check with your false referee, who co-signs the form together with a copy of the photograph to confirm your identity. But, as Peter soon realised—this rarely happened. Therefore, as long as you used a valid address which can be checked on the Electoral Register, the application will be processed and a genuine passport issued with the false name and address. It was that simple, providing you had the funds to pay for it – and Peter had that in abundance. Peter had no regrets about Petrie's death. After all, Petrie had threatened his family and that was all the justification that Peter needed to satisfy himself that he had done the right thing.

Chapter 4

The metallic grey Ford Mondeo pulled into the driveway leading up to the home of Michael Donaldson, MSP. It was a beautiful detached red sandstone property with an adjoining double garage. Claire assumed the garage had been added later but nevertheless was impressed by the overall condition of the building. Unlike some buildings of a similar age, the owners of this one had clearly spent a lot of money maintaining it over the years.

"How can a politician afford a place like this?" asked Brian as he stopped the car outside the large entrance to the house. "I didn't think they were paid that much."

"They're not. Maybe he inherited it," suggested Claire, "or perhaps it belongs to his wife."

The front door opened before they could get out of the car. An anxious-looking woman stood there, her arms crossed protecting her from the cold. Claire looked up and waved to her before approaching the stairs. Claire couldn't help but notice that the woman was in her mid-thirties and was extremely attractive: she had long brown hair, a slim waistline and was well dressed in expensive clothing. Not quite what Claire had expected as the MSP was at best in his late fifties, or so he had appeared in various images on the internet. *Could it be his daughter?* Claire wondered.

"Hi, I'm Detective Inspector Claire Redding and this is Detective Sergeant Brian O'Neill." Claire extended her hand to offer a handshake, but the woman declined it.

"I'm Mrs Donaldson. Please come in," she said curtly and then turned back towards the house. She led the two detectives into a room on the right-hand side of the impressive hallway. As Claire entered the brightly lit room, she admired the beautiful windows and exquisite decoration. *So this is how the other half live*, she thought.

Brian was equally impressed and marvelled at the high ceilings and ornate coving.

"Please, take a seat Inspector... sorry what was your name again?"

"Redding. Claire Redding and this is DS Brian O'Neill."

Mrs Donaldson looked dismissively at Brian and then turned back to face Claire. There was an awkward pause as both detectives expected some sort of response or acknowledgement from the woman sitting facing them, but it didn't come. Claire decided to break the ice and Brian removed his notebook from his pocket, ready to take some notes. "Mrs Donaldson, I understand your husband has gone missing?"

"Yes, why else would you be here?" she said sharply.

Blimey, she is a nippy sweetie, thought Brian.

Claire ignored her rudeness and pushed on. "Yes, of course. When was the last time you saw him?"

The woman appeared to relax a little and responded to the question. "Just before I went to bed. It must have been about ten thirty. Mike was in his study, working on his laptop as usual.

I popped in to say goodnight and then went up to bed. I read for a short while and then fell fast asleep. When I woke up this morning, he was gone. He hadn't come to bed. I went downstairs to look for him—to see if he had fallen asleep on the couch."

"In this room?" asked Brian.

"No, this is the guest room. We have a small living room at the back of the house with a television. I've heard some people refer to such rooms as a snug. You know, like on those dreadful house programmes on the television. Anyway, the couches in there are more comfortable than these for lying on," she explained.

"And he wasn't there or anywhere else in the house?" asked Claire.

"No. I checked everywhere. He had disappeared."

Claire nodded. "Right... and were the doors of the house locked?"

"What?" asked Mrs Donaldson, who seemed to be taken aback by what appeared to be a very simple question.

"The front and back doors to the house, did you notice if they were locked?" Claire explained.

"The front door was locked. I had to open it to let you in but I didn't think to check the back one. Why? Is it important?"

It was Claire's turn to be surprised by the question. "Well, if the back door was not locked, is it possible that your husband woke up early from the couch in the living room and has simply gone out for a walk?"

The penny dropped. "Oh, I see what you're getting at. Em…m, no, I didn't think to check the door but surely he would have come home before now. And he would usually leave me a note to say that he had gone out. We have a magnetic notepad on the fridge but there was nothing there this morning. I checked."

Claire nodded in understanding. "So, what time was it when you got up this morning?"

"I always set the alarm for eight on a Monday as I play tennis at nine, with some friends."

Now that Claire had covered most of the easy questions and Mrs Donaldson appeared to be talking freely, she decided to change direction. "Mrs Donaldson, I'm afraid I need to ask you some personal questions about your relationship with your husband. Is that okay?"

"Why?" she asked indignantly.

"Well, with every missing person investigation, it helps if we have the full background on the person that we're looking for."

"Oh, I see. Yes, well, if you must."

"Thank you. How would you describe your relationship with your husband at the moment?"

"It's fine. Normal, I suppose," she responded cautiously.

"So you have no reason to believe that your husband may be seeing someone else?"

"No, and I take offence to that suggestion, Inspector," she snapped.

Claire remembered the warning that the DCI had given to her before leaving the station. *Be careful*. "Mrs Donaldson, I'm sorry if the *question* offended you but I'm only trying to establish if your husband might have gone somewhere without your knowledge. The more information we gather the easier it will be for us to find him. I hope you understand."

The woman shuffled in her chair and nodded.

Claire continued. "For example, could your husband have gone into his office early? An emergency perhaps?"

"I've checked with his Personal Assistant—he's not there and he's not called in either."

This prompted Claire's next question. "I assume your husband has a mobile phone?"

"Yes, he has two—one for his office and his personal one."

"And I assume you have tried calling both numbers?" asked Claire.

"Yes, of course I did, I'm not stupid. They both went straight to his answer phone. I have called both numbers several times and left numerous text messages."

Claire ignored her rudeness and carried on. "Okay, if you provide DS O'Neill with those numbers, we can try and trace both phones. Hopefully, that will tell us where he is."

Claire tried to think if there was anything that she had missed when Brian kindly interjected. "Does he have a car?"

"Yes, a green Jaguar. It's in the garage alongside my Range Rover, I checked this morning. There's a door directly off the kitchen which connects to the garage. We had the garage built when we first moved in. The Council insisted that the exterior matched the red sandstone of the main building, which cost a bloody fortune, but at least they granted permission in the end. Well, they had to, after all, Mike is a senior member of the government."

Brian had wondered how long it would take before she mentioned it. He did not like the woman and his initial sympathy for her was dwindling. Claire was just grateful for the extra time to come up with some more questions—she was clearly a bit rusty after her time off to recover.

"Is there anywhere else that your husband could be Mrs Donaldson? Somewhere else he might have gone. Other family?" asked Claire, taking over again.

"No, both his parents are dead and we don't have any children."

"No siblings?"

"Well, Mike has a younger brother, David, who lives in Glasgow but they don't get on. They fell out when Mike bought this house from his parents a few years ago. His parents were too old to maintain the house and wanted to move into a flat, which they did but eventually—they had to go into residential care and used the money from the house to pay for it. David was raging when he found out; he was expecting to inherit half the proceeds from the sale of the house when his parents passed but it didn't turn out that way."

"Right, we'll need to check with him, so if you can give DS O'Neill, David's contact information that would be helpful."

While Brian jotted down the details, Claire stood and looked out of the large bay window into the gardens, which she noted were very well maintained. "Do you do all the gardening yourself?" she asked casually.

"No, we have a gardener who comes round once a week, on a Friday."

Claire nodded to herself and then turned back to face Mrs Donaldson. "Can you show us the study where you last saw your husband?"

Mrs Donaldson stood up and headed for the door. "Of course, follow me."

She led both detectives to a small room on the other side of the house. Opened the door and stood back to let them enter. "I'll just go and check the back door."

Claire entered the room first. It was quite different from the beautiful guest room they had just left. The walls were lined with oak wood panelling which also framed a small window at the back of the room. A solid oak desk with a black leather chair sat proudly in front of the small window. To her right, Claire glanced at a huge bookcase that took up most of the wall and to her left there was a small drinks table. It had a round silver tray with a crystal decanter which was half full of a golden spirit—probably whisky—and some crystal shot glasses on the side.

There was a laptop sitting open on the desk and Claire immediately went to see if it was still on, but it wasn't. Claire also noted that there was a brown leather briefcase and a black laptop bag lying on the floor—further evidence that Donaldson had not gone to his office that morning. Claire checked that the window was locked. *No sign of entry or exit and no sign of a struggle,* thought Claire, looking around, trying to find anything unusual or out of the ordinary, but there was nothing. The room was spotless.

Brian checked the bookcase which, among other things, had an eclectic mix of biographies of famous politicians such as Churchill, Major, Blair, Obama and Alex Salmond—the former leader of the Scottish National Party.

"Find anything useful?" asked Mrs Donaldson as she entered the room. Claire turned and shook her head. "Not really, but it would be good to know what he was working on last night," she said, pointing to the laptop. "You wouldn't happen to know his password?"

"No, sorry, I don't. His PA might be able to help with that. He's on his way over now. Oh, and the back door wasn't locked."

"So he could have gone for a walk then," said Claire. "Does he have a favourite walking route or path that he prefers?"

Mrs Donaldson paused before responding. "Yes, there's a path which leads all the way to Glen Fruin. It starts just behind the Hill House and goes along towards Rhu, overlooking the town, and then cuts back over to the glen. We often walk that way on weekends."

"Right, we'll get some officers to check out the path. He might have fallen and hurt himself. Brian, can you call it in while I have a quick look round the rest of the house?"

"No problem, Boss." Brian did as he was told and called the station.

Chapter 5

Peter sat nervously at his desk. He picked up his phone and made the call. A gruff voice answered. "Hello!"

"Mr Baxter?" asked Peter.

"Yes, who is this?"

Peter was not about to identify himself and had prepared a response. "We've done business before... involving Petrie."

"Oh, it's you. I thought I told you *not* to call me again. In fact, I *warned* you not to call me again," he growled down the line.

"I know and you did, but I have another offer to make."

"And what would that be?" asked Baxter, now showing more interest in the call.

"I need some information and think you can help me get it."

"Is that right? What information would that be?"

"I need to know who ordered the hit on Detective Inspector Claire Redding."

"Well, that's easy. It was Petrie. I thought everyone and their auntie knew that!" His sarcasm dripped from every word.

"No, I know he was responsible but I want to know who it was within his organisation that carried out the instruction. Someone on the outside must have been involved and I want to know who."

"Well, I'm afraid you're barking up the wrong tree there, pal."

"What do you mean?" asked Peter.

"I have taken over Petrie's business, and everyone who worked for him, now works for me. So let me give you another wee word of warning. Drop this fuckin' futile search for someone to blame and focus on looking after that wee woman of yours."

Peter was shocked by Baxter's revelation. "What? What do you mean?"

"Listen, son, do you think I'm stupid. Do you think that I'd enter into business with a complete stranger? I know who you are... Peter MacDonald, I know where you live, and I know who you live with. Can I make myself any clearer son? So listen carefully—you do not call me again, you do not ask any more questions about who helped Petrie on the outside. Do you understand?"

Peter gulped before speaking. "Yes, I understand." Peter was shell-shocked. *How the hell did Baxter know my name? This was bad. Really bad!*

Baxter hung up the phone and swore out loud.

"Trouble boss?" asked McCafferty, one of Petrie's former employees.

"Not yet, but I don't think that's the last time I'm going to hear from Peter fuckin' Macdonald! We'll need to keep an eye on that wee fucker."

Chapter 6

Claire and Brian were back in the police station in Dumbarton. The search of the house had proven to be fruitless and now the search for the missing Government minister was really kicking off. Assistant Chief Constable Blackford had already been on the phone to DCI Morrison twice that morning and unsurprisingly news of the missing MSP was beginning to spread throughout the media. Morrison could feel an almighty headache coming on—she had every officer available out looking for him and had assigned two teams to search the path between Glen Fruin and Helensburgh, each team at opposite ends of the route in the hope of finding him before they met somewhere in the middle.

Brian was in the CID room busy typing up the report, while Claire was in DCI Morrison's office, giving her a verbal update on the interview with Mrs Donaldson. The DCI bristled with annoyance when Claire told her that Mrs Donaldson had been upset when she asked about her husband having an affair.

"I thought I told you to be careful. For goodness' sake, Claire. The poor woman's husband has gone missing and you're accusing him of having an affair? No wonder she was upset."

"I only asked the question. I didn't accuse him of anything!" Claire protested.

"Well, let's hope that she doesn't make a complaint. The Chief Super is already concerned about the level of attention this case is bringing our way, not to mention ACC Blackford."

Claire smiled at the memory of ACC Blackford's disastrous media briefing on the serial killings. "I hope they keep her away from the media!" she joked.

"This is not a laughing matter, Claire. If we don't find Donaldson soon, I can't imagine the ..." She was interrupted by the phone ringing on her desk which she promptly answered. "DCI Morrison here. Yes. You have? Good. Where? What? Oh shit! Right, I'm on my way."

Claire stared at the DCI. "They've found him?"

"Yes, but he's dead. The constable who found him thinks it's suicide—he's hanging from a tree. You were right to have the path searched because that's exactly where they found him. Come on, grab your jacket."

Claire didn't need to be asked twice and was already on her way back to the office.

"And tell Brian, he's in charge until we get back," Morrison shouted along the corridor.

~

Peter was in complete turmoil again. His plan to involve Baxter had backfired and he was struggling to come up with a better plan. He had to find out who was responsible for his child's death and make them pay. And while Baxter's warning had sent a chill down his spine, it had not been enough to put him off. No, he had to do something and then a thought suddenly occurred to him. He started to type on his laptop and quickly found what he wanted—a list of Private Investigators in the Glasgow area. Why hadn't he thought of this before now? He called the first number on the list and waited for it to be answered.

Chapter 7

DCI Morrison and DI Redding arrived at the spot where Mike Donaldson's body was hanging limp from a bough of the tree.

The latter part of the journey from the station had been a rough one as the two detectives had to use a Land Rover to get near the site, and even then they had to walk some of the way as the path was too narrow and the ground too soft to support the vehicle.

They identified themselves and then made their way through the cordon of blue and white police tape and headed towards the body, the silhouette of which was clearly visible against the brightly lit southern sky. Even though his eyes were closed and his skin had taken on a pale greyish-blue colour, she knew it was him. It was Donaldson. She looked down and noticed something on the ground, glinting in the late morning sunshine. "What's that?" she said and bent down to take a closer look.

"What?" asked Morrison, whose attention had been focussed on the hanging body. She looked down and could now see what Claire had spotted. A coin. A small silver coin, and then as she looked more carefully, there were others, scattered all over the ground.

"Right, no one goes near the body until the Scene of Crime team gets here," Morrison instructed.

"What are you thinking?" asked Claire.

"Well, either they've fallen out his pocket or whoever put him up there has dropped them. Either way, they might contain fingerprints or some other clue as to what has happened here."

Claire nodded in agreement and stared up at the tree, trying to envisage how it could have happened. *How did he get up there?*

The rope had been wrapped around the third bough which was about ten feet off the ground. Then, it had been tied to the lowest branch on the opposite side of the trunk, which was low enough to reach from ground level.

There was another smaller branch about three feet above it but it didn't look strong enough to support anything, let alone a man. "If it were suicide, he would need to have thrown the rope up onto the third bough first, adjusted the height, wrapped it round, and then tied the rope off. He would then have to climb up to the third bough, put the noose around his neck and then drop down," said Claire, pointing to each bough as she described her thought process.

Morrison played out the scenario in her head and then nodded. "Yip, it's possible. However, I think we're going to need to wait for the pathologist's report before we'll know the actual cause of death. I've never seen a hanging before. Have you?"

"No, it's a first for me," said Claire.

"Well, I've seen enough here. You wait until the SOC team and the pathologist arrive. Shouldn't be too long—Doctor McAlpine is already on his way. Keep in touch and if there are any major developments let me know. And text me if you can't get through—my phone is going to be busy! This is as high profile as it gets so we can expect a lot of scrutiny on this one!"

Great! That's all I need! Claire looked further up the hill and could see some press photographers gathering outside the cordon, their long-distance lenses focussing on the body. *Shit!*

She barked some orders out to two Uniforms who had been assigned to patrol the perimeter and made them extend the cordon further up the field, but it was too little too late. She knew the images would be out there on social media within minutes such was the miracle of modern communication.

Claire turned back to the body again. This time, her thoughts travelled in another direction. *If it wasn't suicide then how did the killer get the body up here and how did they manage to hang him up there?* Donaldson wasn't a big man by any standards, but he looked to weigh at least thirteen stone, maybe more. Claire concluded that if it wasn't suicide then whoever did this must have been strong and had a vehicle suitable for driving on rough terrain—something like the Police Land Rover she had used, or better still, a tractor.

She decided to walk all the way around the tree, being careful not to tread on any of the coins that lay scattered on the ground. That's when she noticed that the bottom of Donaldson's trousers were dirty—the brown mud had all but dried in but she could still make out the contrast of colour. She took a mental note to get the SOCO to take close-up photographs of that area before lowering the body to the ground. She looked at her watch and sighed. She hated waiting.

Chapter 8

Just as DCI Morrison had predicted, Dr McAlpine, the Lead Pathologist based in the Glasgow Mortuary arrived on the scene shortly after the DCI's departure. He was wearing a beige woollen coat, brown slacks and a pair of black ankle boots. As usual, he was carrying a small leather bag which contained the basic implements required for the examination of a dead body.

McAlpine was a very experienced pathologist and although his overgrown ego would never let him admit it, he was close to his official retirement age. Not that it mattered much, as age was often less of a barrier to a successful career than lack of ability. Some would say that he was very old-fashioned and stuck in his ways but Claire just thought he was rude and very unlikeable. He had not made her first post-mortem examination an easy affair and had been quite dismissive of the young detective. However, her reputation had grown quite considerably since then and his attitude towards her had mellowed. That said, he was still a pompous ass as far as Claire was concerned.

"Detective Inspector Redding, or should I say MacDonald?" he smirked. "I understand you are married now."

"DI Redding is just fine," said Claire, unwilling to engage in any frivolous conversation with the disagreeable physician.

"A modern woman! Keeping your own name. What does hubby think about that?"

"As a matter of fact, he's fine with it.," said Claire, smiling back at McAlpine's smug face.

He turned and faced the hanging body. "So this is our high-profile government minister? How the mighty have fallen! Pardon the pun!"

Claire ignored his weak attempt at humour. "Yes, and I'm afraid you'll have to wait for the SOC team to get here before you can examine him."

"Yes, I passed them on the way in—they were unloading their van when I arrived. The poor sods will have to carry all their gear up here."

Claire nodded, "Yes, it's not the most accessible spot. Is it?"

"No, but I know it quite well. I live in Helensburgh."

"I didn't know that. Whereabouts?"

"Not far from the victim's home, actually."

"Really? Did you know him?" asked Claire, who was no longer just making polite conversation. Perhaps she could learn something useful from McAlpine.

"Well, not really, not personally, I mean. Some of my friends know…, sorry… knew him and let's just say that he was not popular around these parts. Of course, he's a politician and that goes with the territory, but if you go about publicly supporting the removal of the naval base in what is effectively a naval town, then you're bound to make a few enemies. Let's face it— half the population of Helensburgh either work at the base or their businesses rely on its employees for custom."

Claire knew McAlpine was referring to the Clyde Naval Base at Faslane and Coulport, home to the fleet of British nuclear submarines, and a major employer in the area. "That's very interesting," said Claire.

"Do you know what else is interesting?" asked McAlpine.

"No, but I'm sure you're going to enlighten me if I wait around long enough," said Claire sarcastically.

"That tree..." he paused, deliberately building the tension.

"Go on, don't keep me hanging!" Claire urged, her curiosity now getting the better of her.

"Good one... hanging, that's funnier than mine."

"That wouldn't be difficult," said Claire. "So, what's so interesting about the tree?"

McAlpine beamed. "Might be a coincidence, but it is known locally as the 'Judas Tree!'"

"What?" As in the bible? Why?"

"Well, look at it Inspector, it's the perfect tree for hanging oneself, don't you think?"

Claire's mind was already working at pace. *Judas, silver coins, betrayal... a message perhaps... or possibly a motive?*

Chapter 9

Peter's search for a private investigator was proving to be much more difficult than he had first envisaged. As soon as he mentioned the name Petrie, they were suddenly unable to assist him. He had even resorted to offering them double their normal rate as an incentive, but so far no one was willing to help. He decided to start from the bottom of the list in the hope that they might be more desperate for business than those on the top. He dialled the number and waited for an answer. After a couple of rings an Irish male voice answered. Peter guessed he must have been from the South as his accent was soft and not harsh like the North.

"McKinley's Investigations. Can I help you?"

"I hope so," said Peter and went on to explain the information he needed about Petrie. This time the investigator didn't stop Peter in his tracks or end the call. He listened carefully to what Peter had to say before responding.

"Okay, so you want to know who was involved on the outside. Is that right?" asked McKinley.

"Yes, that's all," said Peter, sensing that the investigator was interested.

"And what do you intend to do with the information?"

"Give it to the Police," Peter lied.

"And the Police have investigated this already and have found nothing? I mean, I'd have thought they would have gone all out to track these people down, given it was one of their own who got hurt"

"Well, they did and they have their suspicions but couldn't find any evidence," Peter explained.

"And they wouldn't tell you who they suspected?"

"No, but they did say, off the record, that Petrie's lawyer might have been involved as he was the only one to visit him in prison."

"Yeah, well, there are other ways to get a message out of a jail, you know."

"No, I don't know."

"Okay, so this fella, Petrie, could have bribed a guard to pass a message on and the guard might not even know what the message was about. Or someone could sneak a mobile phone into the prison to let Petrie make the call in private. I'm not surprised that the Police couldn't pin anything on the lawyer."

"Oh!" said Peter, unable to hide his disappointment.

"Listen, young fella, I can't make any promises but I have a few contacts at Barlinnie. I'll ask around and see what I can find out for you. How's that?"

Peter was disappointed but felt he had no option but to agree. "Yes, I suppose so. How much do you want?"

"We can talk about that if I find anything and if I don't then there will be no charge. Is that okay Mr... sorry I didn't catch your name?"

"Davidson, Thomas Davidson. Yes, that sounds very reasonable," said Peter.

"And is it okay for me to call you back on this number?"

"Yes," said Peter. "So how quickly do you think you can get back to me?"

"Depends how quickly I can get hold of my contact. Shouldn't take too long but I should warn you, I might have to pay him something for his trouble—you know, keep him sweet."

"Not a problem," said Peter. "Whatever it takes."

"Good. Some of my clients seem to have a problem paying out for bribes but it's a necessary part of the business and anyone who tells you different is a liar."

"As I said, it's not a problem," Peter repeated. He ended the call and then smiled to himself. *At last, he was finally getting somewhere!*

Chapter 10

After the SOC Team and pathologist had finished their work and the body had been removed from the scene, Claire made her way back to the station and headed straight to DCI Morrison's Office to give her an update on her findings. To her surprise, a familiar face was waiting for her in the DCI's Office.

"Hello, Claire," said DCI Carter, as she entered the room.

Claire had worked with Carter from the Major Incident team on a recent serial killer case. "Hello, sir," she responded. "What brings you back here?"

"Take a seat, Claire," said Morrison, pointing to the empty chair opposite her. "Given the high-profile nature of this case, and now that we have what appears to be a suspicious death on our hands, the Chief Constable has decided that MIT should assist us with this investigation."

"Assist with the investigation? What does that mean?" Claire asked, looking at her DCI and then at Carter.

"It means exactly that, Claire," said Carter. "We're not taking over the case as such, but a few members of my team have been assigned to assist with the investigation. The powers-to-be want a quick resolution, and as you know, MIT has access to more resources than CID."

Claire nodded slowly, conveying her agreement; the MIT was better resourced to deal with murder investigations should her suspicions be confirmed. Claire also knew there was no point arguing as the decision had already been taken at the very top. "I see, sir. So how is this going to work?"

"We'll use the incident room that's already set up here. I'll take over as SIO and I'll bring in Rambo and Doyle from my team to support your guys."

Rambo, DS Ramnik Bahanda, an ICT expert, and DC Doyle had worked with Claire on the previous case. Doyle, the most inexperienced member of the team, had been removed from the case when he inadvertently shared some protected information with the British Transport Police. "What about Woody? Who is going to run the incident room?"

"I was hoping Brian would be up for that role," Carter replied, knowing full well that would please Claire.

"I'm sure he'd be happy to do it," said Claire, clearly warming to the idea.

"Good," said Carter. "So why don't you start by giving DCI Morrison and me an update on your findings at the scene."

"Yes, of course, sir. The pathologist can't be sure until he carries out the post-mortem examination, but he believes that Mr. Donaldson may have been dead before he was hanged. His initial inspection of the body suggested that the rope marks around the neck indicated that the body had been pulled up by the rope as opposed to him dropping down from a height. This theory is also consistent with the findings of the SOC Team who found some friction marks on the tree bough, which also suggests that the body was pulled up off the ground. Of course, that alone does not mean that he was dead before he was hanged. He could have been pulled up there to hang while still alive. However, given the apparent lack of visible burst blood vessels around the neck area, Dr McAlpine was confident that his heart had stopped pumping blood before he was hanged," explained Claire.

"So, not suicide then," said Carter.

"Shit," exclaimed Morrison.

Claire and Carter turned simultaneously to face Morrison, whose face had turned pale. "The Chief Super has already been out to see Mrs Donaldson and told her that it was probably suicide!"

"What! Why?" asked Claire.

"I think she felt under pressure to give her some explanation, and at the time I had told her that it could have been suicide."

"Great, someone will have to go and tell her that we now suspect foul play," said Claire. She looked up and could see both sets of eyes were on her.

"Wait! I'm not sure I'm the best person to break the news. She didn't warm to me this morning."

Carter turned to Claire. "It's okay, we'll do it together. And to be totally honest, we still won't know for sure that it was foul play until we get the post-mortem results. So, we can gently introduce the notion that there could have been someone else involved in his death and we have some more questions which need to be answered as part of the investigation."

Claire was impressed by Carter's response—this was a different DCI compared to the rough and ready version she had encountered on their previous case. Of course, they were after a brutal serial killer at that point and were under severe pressure to catch him. This case was different and would need a more sensitive approach. Claire continued with her update. "According to Dr McAlpine, there could be a lengthy list of people with good reason to get rid of Donaldson. Apparently, he wasn't popular in the town. Even his brother doesn't speak to him."

"Is that right?" asked Carter.

"Yes, according to Mrs Donaldson, they fell out over the family home, which her husband had bought from his parents, stripping the brother of any chance of getting a share of the house as inheritance."

"Now, that is a motive," said Carter. "We'll need to interview the brother as soon as we've finished with the wife."

"There's something else, sir," said Claire. "Thirty pieces of silver!"

"What?"

"Under the tree. The SOC team confirmed that there were thirty silver coins on the ground underneath the body."

"Jesus!" Carter exclaimed.

"No, 'Judas' actually. According to Dr McAlpine, who lives in Helensburgh, the tree is known locally as the Judas Tree because, in his words, it's perfect for hanging oneself."

"McAlpine! I remember now, is he that pompous prick from the Glasgow mortuary?" asked Carter.

Claire smiled and nodded. "Yip! That's the one."

"So that suggests betrayal then; someone wants it to be known that Donaldson betrayed them and has paid the price?"

"Looks that way, yes," said Claire. "And probably someone local… or was brought up in the area."

Carter nodded. "Like the younger brother who also happens to have a good motive. Right, he goes to the top of the list of suspects for now, but let's go and interview the wife first and find out who else might have a motive to kill him."

"There's also his Personal Assistant, sir."

"What? He has a motive as well as the brother?"

"Sorry, no, but he might be able to give us some insight on what the Minister was working on and if there's anything of political importance that we should know. There could be a lot of people who could benefit from Donaldson's death, not to mention his wife who will inherit the house."

"No stone unturned, Inspector!" said Carter.

"Yes, sir. No stone unturned." This had become their new motto.

DCI Morrison didn't get the significance of Carter's comment but assumed it must have been a reference to their previous case. "Okay, I'll let Brian and the others know what is happening. You two should head off and speak to Mrs Donaldson, without delay. Carter, when can we expect to receive the other two team members?"

"They should be on their way now," he replied, checking his watch. "And should get here within the next ten minutes or so."

"Right, I'll need to make sure we have sufficient desks and chairs for them," said Morrison, getting to her feet and indicating that the meeting was over. "And I'll assign a couple of uniforms to assist you."

"Great," said Carter. "Come on, Claire."

They headed down to the car park and made a beeline for Carter's car. However, before he opened the doors, Carter stopped and faced Claire. "Claire, I'm sorry about... the baby. Must have been tough on you... and Peter."

It suddenly occurred to Claire that for the first time in twelve weeks, she hadn't thought about the loss of the baby that day. This case was exactly what she needed. "Yes, yes it was," she replied.

"Are you sure you are up for this?" There was genuine concern on his face.

"Try and stop me," she said, grinning.

"Good, let's go then."

Chapter 11

Carter's car pulled into the long driveway leading up to the Donaldsons' house. Claire had briefed Carter on the previous interview on the road to Helensburgh.

"When you said she'd inherit the house, I didn't realise it was a bloody stately home," quipped Carter, taking in the grandeur of the property facing him. "It must be worth a fortune."

Claire didn't respond to his remarks. "I think you should take the lead on this one, sir. As I said, Mrs Donaldson didn't really warm to me the first time round and now that her husband is dead…"

"Not a problem, but if you feel you want to jump in, do so."

He parked the car behind a red Ford Fiesta, which was also parked on the driveway but not obstructing the staircase. It belonged to PC Jenny Barnes, Family Liaison Officer. As if by magic, the large door of the house opened just as they climbed up the steps to the house. Jenny had seen them arrive from the front window.

"Hello Jenny," said Claire as she entered the house. "This is DCI Carter."

Jenny stepped back to allow both detectives to enter the hallway and then closed the door. "Hello, sir. I don't think we've met before."

Carter smiled. "No, I don't believe we have, constable. Where is Mrs Donaldson?"

Jenny pointed to the same room that Claire had been in before. "She's in the guest room. Can I get you some tea or coffee? I put the kettle on for Mrs Donaldson a few minutes ago."

"That would be great," said Claire who realised suddenly that she had had nothing to eat or drink since breakfast.

"Some biscuits would be good," said Carter, reading Claire's mind.

"I'll see what I can do," said Jenny, grinning up at the DCI and then heading off in the direction of the kitchen.

Carter and Claire entered the guest room where Mrs Donaldson was sitting and waiting for them to appear. She stood up as they entered.

"Mrs Donaldson, I'm Detective Chief Inspector Carter from the Major Incident Team. I believe you've met DI Redding from Dumbarton CID?"

"Yes, she was here this morning," Mrs Donaldson replied coldly. "What I don't understand is why you are here at all. Chief Superintendent Ralston has already told me that my husband was found hanging from a tree and that it was probably suicide."

Carter looked awkwardly at Claire and then back to Mrs Donaldson, who was still standing. "Perhaps we should all sit down and we'll explain exactly where we are with the investigation at the moment." He looked around and then sat down on the couch facing Mrs Donaldson.

Claire joined him, but Mrs Donaldson remained on her feet.

"Investigation, what do you mean? I thought it was…"

"Please, Mrs Donaldson, take a seat and we'll explain," said Carter. He waited until she was safely sitting down before continuing to speak.

"Thank you. First of all, please understand that with every suspicious death, there will be an investigation to determine whether or not any foul play was involved. In your husband's case, we will need to see the pathologist's report before we can be absolutely certain. Did Chief Superintendent Ralston explain that there would be a post-mortem examination to identify the cause of death?"

"Yes, and that I will need to formally identify the body, but I thought it was just a formality, given that my husband was found hanging."

"I'm afraid not," said Carter. "In fact, DI Redding has been at the scene and her initial investigation suggests there may have been someone else involved." Carter paused to allow Mrs Donaldson to absorb this new piece of information. Her reaction was, as expected, one of shock.

"You mean someone killed Mike. Oh my God!" she exclaimed.

Claire felt that she had to clarify the point. "Mrs Donaldson, we are only saying there *may* have been some foul play and we won't know for sure until we get…"

"The report. Yes, I get it, Inspector. And when will the report be available?" she snapped.

Carter could see that the woman obviously had a problem with Claire and decided he better intervene before the situation became even more heated. "Mrs Donaldson, I can assure you that this case is being given the highest priority. The post-mortem will take place tonight, and we should have the final written report within a day or two, but we'll likely know before then. The pathologist would normally give us early warning if he were sure that a crime has been committed."

Mrs Donaldson nodded slowly. "So, what happens now?"

Before Carter could respond, Jenny entered the room carrying a large tray with two pots: one for tea and one for coffee, as well as some cups, milk and sugar. She laid it down on the coffee table to the right of Claire and invited them to help themselves. Carter noted with annoyance that there were no biscuits on offer. They helped themselves to tea and coffee and then, to Carter's pleasure, Jenny returned with some biscuits, which she laid them on the table and then left the room. Carter immediately lent over Claire to take a handful of biscuits and bumped the arm which was holding her cup. Thankfully, she managed to stop it from spilling onto her coat.

"Oops!" said Carter before stuffing one of the biscuits into his mouth.

Mrs Donaldson gave him a withering look. "You were going to explain what happens next, Chief Inspector?"

"Hmmn," he mumbled, trying to clear the dry biscuit from his palette and then slurping down some tea to help the process.

Claire decided to step in before he tried to speak and choke himself. "I'm afraid that we have some more questions for you, now that we're dealing with a suspicious death rather than a missing person."

"For me? Why? You don't think I had anything to do with it, do you?"

Carter cleared his throat and took over again. "No, of course not. What we really want to know is who would want to kill your husband, if that is what happened here. Did he have any enemies? DI Redding mentioned that Mr Donaldson had fallen out with his brother – or rather his brother had fallen out with him over the house."

"Yes, that's true but I don't think David would hurt Mike… and it was some time ago."

"What about others? He must have had a few political enemies?" Carter prompted.

"I'm sure he did, but I'm not the best person to ask that question. His PA, Malcolm Munro, would probably be able to ask about that sort of stuff."

"Yes, we'll need to speak to him," Carter confirmed.

The mention of the name prompted Claire to cut in. "Earlier today you said that Mr Munro was on his way here. Is he still here?"

"No, he picked up a few of Mike's things and left."

"What things?" asked Claire.

"His laptop and briefcase. Apparently, it contained some confidential government papers, so Malcolm thought it could be safer for him to look after them until Mike turned up. Obviously, he didn't know that Mike was dead at that point," she added.

"Of course," said Carter. "But we'll need to get those items back as they may be relevant to the investigation."

"Well, I imagine he'll be halfway to Edinburgh by now. He left about an hour ago."

"Do you have his mobile number?" asked Carter.

Claire interrupted before Mrs Donaldson could reply. "No need, sir. DS O'Neill has his number. I'll call him and get him to contact Mr Munro. Hopefully, we'll get him back to the station for questioning and take possession of the laptop and briefcase."

"Take possession? I'm not sure you can do that. It's government property. Do you not need to get a warrant or something?"

Carter responded. "It depends on whether this is a murder investigation or not. If it is, then those items will be held as evidence. If not, then they will be returned. On that particular point, I understand that you last saw your husband alive in his office. Is that correct?"

"His study. Yes, as I have already explained to DI Redding, he was sitting at his desk working on his laptop."

"And DI Redding has checked the rest of the property and there was no sign of a struggle or a break-in."

"Yes, but I don't see…"

"Mrs Donaldson. That all suggests that your husband walked out of here on his own free will," explained Carter.

"Oh, I see, I hadn't thought of that."

"And I wouldn't expect you to. You must still be in shock."

"Yes, shock. That's what it must be," she said quietly.

"If I could ask you not to go into the off... sorry, the study, until our forensic team have examined the room. That would be helpful."

"Why, what do you hope to find in there? DI Redding and the other policeman have already checked it."

"Yes, but there could be some fibres or fingerprints which might help us to identify if anyone else was in the room with your husband last night. We'll also need to take samples of your DNA for elimination purposes. With your permission, of course."

"Oh, I see. Well, if it's absolutely necessary."

"As I said before, this is all just as a precaution in case the pathologist confirms foul play," said Claire.

"But you suspect there was. Why is that Inspector?"

"I'm sorry, but I can't reveal that type of information at the moment, but if our suspicions are confirmed by the pathologist, then perhaps I can share some of my findings with you."

"I suppose I'll have to wait then," she said sulkily.

Chapter 12

The interview ended and Carter and Claire made their way to the door. Jenny followed them outside and closed the door behind her, clearly wanting to have a quick chat with the detectives. "How did it go?" she asked.

Carter continued down the stairs and lit a cigarette while Claire held back to speak to the constable. "As expected, but there weren't any tears," said Claire. "How was she when the Chief Super was here?"

"Very quiet. I put it down to the shock - the tears will come later I suppose, when she's alone and it all sinks in."

"Is that normal? I mean, in the circumstances?"

"There is no normal in these circumstances," said Jenny. "Believe me, I've seen it all."

"Thanks, Jenny. Oh, DCI Carter has asked that no one enter the study until forensics have examined it. Can you make sure Mrs Donaldson doesn't forget?"

"Yes, of course."

Claire made her way downstairs to the car where Carter was standing with a cigarette in hand. "I didn't know you smoked."

Carter could sense the tone of disapproval. He took a final draw, blew out the smoke, threw the stub onto the ground and stood on it. "I gave it up a while ago but after our last case, well… I just started again. Stupid, I know, so no lectures please."

"I wouldn't dream of it, sir," said Claire.

"And you can drop the 'sir' when we're on our own, Claire. Carter is fine."

"Yes, sir," she replied automatically. "Sorry!" Claire looked up at the house. "Well, what do you think about Mrs Donaldson?"

"I don't think she likes you," said Carter with a grin, and slid into the driver seat. "So, where does this brother live then?"

"West End of Glasgow. Just off Byres Road," said Claire, and took out her mobile phone. Brian responded on the second ring. "Hi Brian, we're off to interview David Donaldson, the brother. Can you text me his number? And can you get a hold of Malcolm Munro, Donaldson's P.A. He's heading back to Edinburgh with Donaldson's case and laptop. Yeah, I know – unbelievable! Just get him to come back to the station and let me know when he's there—we want to question him as soon as we're finished with the brother. Oh, and can you get the SOC Team out to Donaldson's house as soon as possible. We want his study checked out for prints and fibres. Get them to take a DNA kit—Mrs Donaldson has agreed to give a sample. Yes, for elimination purposes. Thanks."

Within seconds of hanging up, Claire's phone pinged to indicate a text message had been received. It was Brian texting David Donaldson's number. She immediately called the number. After a few rings, David Donaldson answered the call.

"Hello, is that David Donaldson?"

"Yes, who is this?" he asked politely.

"I'm Detective Inspector Claire Redding. I would like to speak to you about your brother, Michael Donaldson. I assume you have heard."

"That he's dead. Yes, it's all over the media."

"I'm sorry… that you had to find out way," said Claire.

"Are you the policewoman in the photograph?"

"Sorry? What photograph?"

"The one plastered all over social media and the news. Standing in front of the tree."

Claire's stomach turned. "Yes. I'm sorry. We tried to stop them, but they were able to take photographs from further up the hill outside of our cordon."

"Don't worry about it, Inspector. It doesn't bother me. Mike lived his life in front of the camera so it's only fitting that it's the same in death."

No love lost there then, thought Claire. "Are you at home, Mr Donaldson?"

"No, but I'm heading there now."

"Right." She checked her watch. "We should be with you in about 35 minutes, traffic permitting. Is that okay?"

"That's fine. I'll see you then," he said and hung up.

Carter turned to Claire. "So, what do you think?"

"Well, he didn't sound very upset about his brother's death, that's for certain."

"Uh-huh. And what was that about a photograph?"

Claire sighed. "It appears there's a photograph of me standing beside the hanging body and it's all over the bloody media."

"What? Didn't the SOC Team screen it off?"

"They hadn't arrived at that point. Goodness knows how the press got wind of it so quickly. You know I think they must be tapping our phones or something."

"Wouldn't surprise me, but it's more than likely to be one of our boys taking a bung to give them the heads up."

Claire shook her head in dismay. "Do you think we're going to get in trouble for allowing the photo to be taken?"

"A photograph of a dead politician splashed all over social media. A government minister, no less! What do you think?"

Chapter 13

Claire and Carter arrived at David Donaldson's address approximately forty-five minutes after leaving Helensburgh. The traffic on the A82 had been worse than Claire had anticipated, and it appeared that every traffic light on the road beyond Anniesland was triggered to go red just as they approached them. They eventually found a parking space on the busy street and made their way up to the second-floor flat, where David Donaldson lived.

Claire rang the doorbell on the painted wooden door and within seconds it was opened by a younger version of Mike Donaldson. Claire could see the family resemblance; both brothers had similar facial bone structure, with high cheeks and a large forehead. David was taller than his older brother and a good deal thinner. He welcomed both detectives and invited them into the flat. The hall was plainly decorated with cream emulsion paint and the only decorative highlight was a dark blue picture rail.

After brief introductions, David Donaldson led Claire and Carter into what was clearly the living room of the tidy two-bedroom flat and invited them to sit on the only sofa in the room, which faced a traditional black iron fireplace. Claire thought it was a pity that the attractive fireplace was no longer in use as it had been blocked up and tiled over with patterned green tiles. Donaldson sat in a single chair to the right-hand side of the fireplace and faced the detectives.

Carter spoke first. "Before we begin, Mr Donaldson. Can I just say that we're sorry for your loss and that we're grateful that you have agreed to speak to us so soon after news of your brother's death."

"Thank you, Chief Inspector… sorry, what was your name again?"

"Carter. Detective Chief Inspector Carter."

"Yes, of course, sorry—I'm terrible with names. Well, you've probably worked out from my conversation with your colleague that I am not overly upset by news of Mike's death."

"And why is that, may I ask?"

Donaldson responded without hesitation. "Because he was an absolute prick and I despised him."

Carter admired the man's honesty. "Mr Donaldson, before you say anything else, I think you should know that we are treating your brother's death as suspicious."

Donaldson smiled at Carter. "I'm glad to hear it. I never thought for one minute that Mike would kill himself, he doesn't have the balls—sorry didn't have—and that aside, why would he? He had everything going for him. A fantastic job, successful political career, a trophy wife and of course, he got the house." His mood change on the last point was palpable.

"I understand that you were upset when your parents agreed to sell their house to your brother," said Claire keen to explore the motive further.

"That would be an understatement. I was livid. Still am livid. He effectively stole my inheritance," he hissed.

"Yes, but he did pay your parents for the house, and I understand they used the money to fund their care later in life when they were unable to support themselves."

"That's true, but he paid nothing like the full value of the house. In fact, he only paid half but there was nothing I could do about it. They signed over the deeds and that was that."

Claire took a mental note to check how much Mike Donaldson had paid for the house and whether he needed to take out a mortgage to pay for it. Satisfied that the potential motive had been confirmed, Claire decided to change tact. "Mr. Donaldson, do you have any other reason for disliking your brother or was it just the house?"

For the first time, Donaldson hesitated before speaking. It was clear to both detectives that he was mulling over whether to say anything or not.

"Yes, he was a homophobe. Not that you would know it from all the lies he spouted politically. He would say anything to win a few more votes. And, yes, if you hadn't already guessed it, I'm gay."

Claire was taken aback by Donaldson's response. "So, what makes you think he's homophobic?"

Donaldson laughed, but his face wasn't smiling. "You know, I didn't expect my parents to like or even accept it when I told them. After all, they were raised in an era when homosexuality was considered to be a crime committed by deranged queers! Who could blame them? But when my own brother—who I had worshipped up to that point—tells me that he wants nothing more to do with me, that I'm a disgusting pervert... that hurt more than anything. So, I left them all behind and moved here, to Glasgow. You know, I found it ironic that my brother supported the Same-Sex Marriage Act when it went through the Scottish Parliament—what a bloody hypocrite! I was tempted to go public with my story and told him so, but he pleaded with me not to as it would destroy his career. In the end, I decided to let sleeping dogs lie, and what thanks did I get for that? He steals my inheritance."

"Thank you for your openness, Mr Donaldson," said Claire. It couldn't have been easy to share that painful memory with us. You mentioned earlier that your brother had a trophy wife. What did you mean by that?"

"Have you seen her?" Donaldson asked, looking at both detectives. Claire didn't respond. She wanted to hear it from him.

"Well, she's at least twenty years younger than him for a start. He was clearly punching well above his weight."

"So, age aside, how would you describe their relationship?"

"Difficult to say. I barely know her. Mike and I fell out over the gay thing long before they were married and, of course, I wasn't invited to the wedding, but much to his annoyance, I gate-crashed it. Can you imagine? Having to gate-crash my big brother's wedding! Of course, no one other than the happy couple knew it and Mike, keen to prevent a scene, pretended that I had been invited and that the invite must have gone missing in the post. Yeah, right! Anyway, that's the only time I met her—she seemed nice enough and she clearly had no issue with me being gay. It was just Mike."

"Yes, she didn't mention it when we interviewed her," Claire confirmed.

Carter, who had been sitting patiently, had heard enough and decided it was time to bring the interview to an end. "Mr Donaldson, can I ask where you were last night?"

"Of course, I'm a suspect, right? I was here, at home, all night."

"Can anyone confirm that? A partner?"

"No, I'm on my own at the moment."

There was something about the way he said it that made Claire feel sorry for him. He had clearly suffered a lot of personal pain in his life. "One final question, Mr Donaldson. Do you know anyone who would have any reason to want to kill your brother?"

"Sorry, I'm so out of touch now. I wouldn't know who he's dealing with, but what I can say is this. Mike was an arrogant prick, and if the way he treated me was a sign of how he treated others, then there's likely to be a long list."

Claire remembered the conversation she had with McAlpine and nodded. "Thank you."

"Do you have any plans to leave the country over the next few days?" asked Carter.

Donaldson was taken by surprise by the question. "No, why?"

"Because, if you do, we need to know where you are going and why. We may have to bring you in for further questioning."

"So, I am still a suspect."

"Yes. If you had an alibi for the time of the murder then we would be able to eliminate you," Carter confirmed. He didn't see any reason to hide it from Donaldson.

"Should I contact a solicitor?"

"That's your decision, Mr Donaldson, but it would only be necessary if you were arrested or charged with the crime, in which case we would make you fully aware of your rights."

"I see," said Donaldson. "Well, thank you for being so open with me. No offence, but I hope we don't meet again."

Carter smiled at the man. "None taken." There was something about David Donaldson which Carter liked, and deep down, Carter felt a bit sorry for him. *His brother was clearly a prick!*

They said their goodbyes and headed down the tiled staircase to the car. Once inside, Carter turned to Claire. "Well? Gut instinct?"

Claire shook her head. "My gut says no, but if it was him, he's one hell of an actor and that was some performance. What do you think?"

"I wish he had an alibi and we could take him off our list, but as it stands, he has motive and opportunity, so he's still a suspect. Right then, back to Dumbarton. I'm interested to hear what Mr Munro has to say about Michael Donaldson. I get the impression that it won't be complimentary."

Chapter 14

"Hello... Mr Davidson. It's McKinley Investigations. You asked me to help you get some information."

It took Peter a few seconds to remember that he had given Thomas Davidson as a false name. "Yes, sorry. What have you got for me?"

"Okay, I've managed to find out who was acting as Petrie's lawyer while he was in jail," said McKinley.

"Good. Who is it?" asked Peter.

"Not so fast. We need to talk money first."

"Sure, how much do you want?"

McKinley was taken aback by the speed of Peter's response and decided to add another fifty pounds to his bill. "Well, my contact wants one hundred quid, and I want the same. Do we have a deal?"

"Yes, but is that all you have—the name of the lawyer?"

"I'm afraid so. According to my contact, no one else went near the prison, and the search of Petrie's cell did not indicate that he had a mobile phone."

"So, it does look like the lawyer was involved?"

"Yes."

"So, who is he? Do you have a name?"

"I'll text you my bank account details, and once I have received your payment, I'll send you the information. How's that?"

"Fair enough," Peter replied, and ended the call. Within a few minutes, the text came through and he opened his bank app, and sent the cash. Five minutes later, Peter received a text with the solicitor's details. He sat there thinking about how he would approach Wallace and quickly came to a decision.

Chapter 15

Claire and Carter arrived back at the station, where Malcolm Munro was waiting. Brian had put him in interview room two and had offered him some tea or coffee, which he had declined. After quickly speaking with Brian and grabbing a cup of tea each, they made their way to the room. Carter entered first and held the door open for Claire. Munro was sitting, using his mobile phone and immediately put it away when he saw the door open. He was wearing a dark blue pinstripe business suit, grey shirt and yellow tie and looked very fit; his face was well-tanned but not like the orange glow you get from a bottle—it looked more like a healthy outdoor tan, the type golfers acquire through lengthy exposure to sunlight out on the course. He also looked much leaner than the stereotypically fat, lazy civil servant that Carter thought he would be dealing with.

"I'm sorry to have kept you waiting, Mr Munro, but it's been a busy day. I'm Detective Chief Inspector Carter, and this is Detective Inspector Redding. I assume you know why you are here?"

"Yes, I believe you have some questions to ask me about the late Mr Donaldson, MSP."

"That's correct, but first I need to know why you removed Mr Donaldson's laptop and briefcase earlier today?" Carter had decided to go straight for the jugular.

"Well, there were several important confidential documents in his case which I thought should be returned to his office for safekeeping."

"And his laptop?"

"Same reason."

"Right, and you never thought to check with us before doing so?"

"Well… emm… I, eh… I didn't think it would matter," he said, stumbling over his words nervously.

"So, let me get this straight, your boss goes missing and you didn't think what he was working on might be relevant to the investigation?"

"No, I didn't, and as I have just said, there are confidential government papers involved, so I'm not sure you even have the right to see them, never mind keep them. I appreciate the matter is more serious now that Mike... I mean Mr Donaldson has been found dead under suspicious circumstances but I assure you, that's got nothing to do with what he was working on."

"Who said anything about suspicious circumstances?" snapped Carter.

"The First Minister," replied Munro smugly. "The FM received a briefing from the Chief Constable, and his PA made me aware of the situation. I was just reading his text when you came in."

Carter was speechless with rage; it took all his willpower not to throttle the smug-faced Munro, who was sitting opposite him.

"And what was Mr Donaldson working on?" asked Claire, quickly reading the mood and cutting in before Carter said something he would later regret.

"Lots of things. He's Chair of the Economy, Energy and Fair Work Committee." It was said as if Claire and Carter should know all about the machinations of the government and they were expected to stand up and bow in awe of its importance. That wasn't going to happen!

"And what does that Committee do?" asked Claire dismissively.

"It's responsible for all the large infrastructure projects up and down the country. It oversees all the new green environment projects such as wind farms and other large capital projects like the building of new trunk roads and so on," Munro explained, hoping that this would impress the two officers. It didn't, so he decided to hammer home the point. "It's very important and, as both Chair of the Committee and the Minister responsible for that department, Mr Donaldson was at the heart of all major decision making."

"And would you describe any of these projects to be controversial in any way?" asked Claire.

"Oh, I see where you're going with this. You're wondering if any of the projects could be linked to his death."

"Yes," said Claire acerbically. "That is… why we are here."

"Right. Well…eh… the most controversial project in play right now is the relief road planned between Dumbarton and Old Kilpatrick."

Claire had read about this project in the local newspapers; local politicians had been going on for years about the dangers of blockages on the A82, which had resulted in lengthy delays in ambulances getting to the hospitals on the other side of the river. The relief road would offer an alternative route to the A82, other than going via Alexandria and round to Bearsden.

Claire looked puzzled. "Why is that project controversial? I'd have thought it would be great for the people of Dumbarton and Helensburgh to have an alternative road."

"Yes, it will be great for the public and for any business operating in the area. Any improvement to infrastructure indirectly benefits local trade, but it's not so popular with the farmers who own the land on which the road will be built. They have already submitted their objections to the plans and the Committee will likely need to resort to using the compulsory purchase of land, which will be very unpopular with some."

"Any landowners in particular?" asked Claire.

"Well, the farmer standing to lose the most land is James Johnston. The Johnston farm is the biggest in the area, but there are others."

Claire took note of the name and signalled to Carter to continue.

"Mr Munro, we understand that Mr Donaldson was not popular. As his personal assistant, what's your view on that?" asked Carter.

"I'm his *Parliamentary* Assistant!" he said, indignantly. "All government ministers have at least one assigned to them. I am responsible for his department's administration, and as such I am his chief advisor, so we work very closely together."

"A bit like on TV - Yes Minister?" asked Carter.

Munro smiled. "A bit like that, yes, but in a Scottish capacity... obviously. We do things differently up here. Don't get me wrong, Mike also has personal assistants supporting his office, but they're employed by him directly and not by Parliament. He gets to claim expenses to cover the costs."

Claire nodded and brought the conversation back to the original question. "So,

Mr Munro, was the Minister popular? With other politicians, with his staff?"

"Munro paused for a moment before responding. "No, I can't say he was. I... eh... I'm not quite sure if I should mention it but there have been some rumours circulating that he had perhaps been behaving inappropriately with some of the younger female employees."

"Is that so?" asked Carter, prompting Munro to expand on his statement.

"Yes, but it is only a rumour. I'm not aware of any formal complaints. You would need to speak to his staff about it."

"We intend to," said Carter. "We'll need a note of all their names and job titles before you leave. I assume they're all based in Edinburgh?"

"Yes."

Claire sat there quietly trying to comprehend just how many people could have a motive to kill Donaldson. *This case was growing arms and legs by the minute.* And then another possible motive struck her. "Mr Munro, who stands to gain politically now that Mr Donaldson's seat in Parliament has been vacated. Will there be a by-election?"

Carter was glad that Claire had thought to ask that question as up until now he hadn't been thinking in that direction.

"I'm not sure what the process will be as Mr Donaldson was a list MSP."

"A list MSP? What does that mean?" asked Claire.

"There are two types of MSP serving in the Scottish Parliament. It's called the Additional Member System. First of all, you have the Constituency MSPs and they are elected by simple majority or First Past the Post—one for each Scottish Parliamentary Constituency, and then you have the list MSPs who are elected on a regional basis. In Mr Donaldson's case, it would be the West Scotland Region. The list members are elected based on proportional representation, so seats are allocated based on each party's or individual candidate's proportion of the vote. Mr Donaldson stood for the Dumbarton Constituency seat, but lost to the Labour candidate. But as he was top of his party list, he was pretty much guaranteed to win one of the additional seats."

Claire and Carter looked even more confused by this explanation. "So, getting back to the original question, who stands to gain from Mr Donaldson's death?"

"I've no idea. You would need to ask the local election office. It's not really my area of expertise," Munro explained.

"You wouldn't happen to know where that is?" asked Claire.

"Not specifically, but it will be somewhere in your local council offices. The Returning Officer is usually the Chief Executive of the local council."

Claire took a note while Carter tried to think if he had any other questions for Munro and then he remembered. "One last question, Mr Munro, do you know the password to Mr Munro's laptop?"

"No, sorry. And even if I did, I'm not sure I'd be permitted to reveal it."

Carter stood up. "Well, thank you for coming in Mr Munro, you've been extremely helpful. We'll be in touch if we have any further questions. If you can give DI Redding details of Mr Donaldson's staff before you go, that would be great."

"And the names of the other landowners affected by the new road," Claire added.

"Yes, but I'll need to check that when I get back to the office, if that's okay. My memory is not that good and I wouldn't want to miss anyone out."

"Of course," said Claire. "Here's my card with my phone number and email address. The sooner we get the information, the sooner we can check it out."

~

Claire escorted Munro down the stairs to the exit. When she returned to the incident room, she could see that Carter was standing at the incident board talking to Brian. She noticed that a few names had just been added: 'James Johnston (Land)' and 'David Donaldson (Inheritance)' were at the top, the brackets indicating a possible motive. Below those names, Brian had written 'Sexual Harassment' with a large question mark and beside that another question mark with the words 'List Candidates (Vacant Seat).' Below that in bold were the words: JUDAS TREE – COINS (BETRAYAL).

"Should we also add 'Naval base' to the list of motives?" Claire asked. "Dr McAlpine said that Donaldson was outspoken on the issue and wanted to close it down, which was unpopular among the locals."

"That would make every employee a suspect," said Carter.

Claire nodded. "Not to mention local business owners whose trade depends on the base."

Carter shook his head. "I can't see it being a motive for murder though and let's face it—it only becomes a live issue if Scotland votes for Independence. And that's not going to happen any time soon—not now that the Supreme Court has ruled in favour of the UK Parliament's right to veto a referendum." He paused for a moment, scratched his head and then conceded. "Okay, let's put it up there for now so we don't lose sight of it, but I want our focus to be on David Donaldson and James Johnston. They have the strongest motives."

Claire had to agree with Carter on that point; their motives were stronger, but so was that of his political successor. She checked her watch. It was five minutes past five; the council offices would be closed, so the question of who that would be would need to wait until morning.

All three officers stood staring at the board, deep in thought, until Carter broke the silence. "Right, let's get something to eat and then I want to call the team together for a quick update. There's a lot of information to share and a tonne of work to allocate; it's going to be a late night."

Claire took out her phone and texted Peter to let him know that she wasn't coming home for tea.

Chapter 16

Peter was still at his desk when he received the text from Claire. He had been looking at an image of Wallace that he had found on the solicitor's company website. Wallace, Wright and Pratt had an office in Duke Street in the East End of Glasgow. Claire's text made the decision to go and see Wallace an easy one. Hopefully, he could get there and back in time without her realising he had left the house at all. It was perfect timing.

Peter called the office number on the website and asked to speak to Mr Wallace. Within seconds, he was connected to Wallace's

Secretary who apologised and informed Peter that Mr Wallace was with a client. Peter casually asked when Mr Wallace would be available and was told that his current appointment was due to end at 5.30 p.m., but it was unlikely that Mr Wallace would be able to call him back that day as he had other calls to make before the office closed at 6 p.m.

Peter checked his watch. It was 5.15 p.m.; with a little bit of luck, he would get to Wallace's Office just before it closed. This was better than he had hoped as he never intended to confront Wallace in his office in front of witnesses. No, he wanted him on his own. He headed downstairs, locked Sally safely in the kitchen and made his way out the front door to his car.

Chapter 17

The smell of fish and chips in the incident room was overpowering, and even Claire, who normally avoided fast food, was enjoying the free meal that Carter had treated them to as a reward for working late at short notice.

Brian was the only one who had missed out as he had gone home to see Agnes to make her something to eat. Not that she was eating much, but he felt he had to offer her something each night. He had promised to return to the station as soon as possible, so tonight it would just be a ready meal from Morrisons. The spaghetti carbonara could be heated quickly in the microwave and would be ready to serve within five minutes. Perfect for a night like this one.

After they had finished eating, Brian put the dishes in the dishwasher, made sure Agnes had everything she needed and then headed back to the station, just in time for Carter's briefing at 6 p.m.

Content that everyone had finished eating and all fingers had been licked clean of any remaining grease, Carter took centre stage and started the briefing. He quickly summarised the findings from the interviews with Donaldson's wife, his brother and with Munro before inviting Claire to speak. Claire stood up and headed for the board. Carter had asked her if she wanted to share the briefing as he was keen to reinforce the message that it was a joint investigation. She had happily agreed to do so, and was mentally prepared to address the team.

"Thanks, sir. Okay, the initial findings of the pathologist have confirmed that we are dealing with a suspicious death, and it is more than likely that this will be confirmed as a murder case by morning."

She now had their full attention!

Claire waited for the murmurs of excitement to subside and then continued. "The post-mortem is currently underway and there is sufficient evidence to suggest that Donaldson was dead before he was hanged. Dr McAlpine has indicated that, based on body temperature and degree of rigor mortis, the death occurred between the hours of 12 p.m. and 4 a.m., which fits with the statement provided by Mrs Donaldson, who last saw her husband at 10.30 p.m. before she went to bed."

Claire paused for a moment to let the team finish taking down some notes—she was speaking quickly and it was obvious they were struggling to keep up with her. "There was no sign of a struggle in the home, and the backdoor was unlocked, so it's possible Mr Donaldson left the house to go for a walk or to meet someone. What we really need to find out is how did Donaldson end up hanging from the tree? How did he get there, or more importantly how did the killer get him there? It would have taken some strength to haul him up by the rope. And let's not forget that it's an isolated spot along a rough path. Most vehicles would not get far, but a tractor could or perhaps a decent four-by-four. So, does anyone have any thoughts, comments or questions?" asked Claire.

"Was he having an affair?" asked Doyle.

"Good question. I asked his wife the same question when he was first reported as missing and she was quite upset at the suggestion. But that doesn't mean that he wasn't."

"Does the wife have a motive?" asked Rambo.

"Not really, but she does stand to inherit the house and I dare say her husband would have had some life insurance, so that's something we should check. Jim, can you look into it?"

The question was directed at DC Jim Armstrong, who was sitting quietly up the back of the room. "Sure thing, boss," he replied.

"So, as you can see from the board, there are several people with a motive to kill Donaldson; he appears to have more enemies than Putin," she quipped. There was a ripple of laughter around the room.

Claire turned and pointed to the board. "There's his brother who despised him. The farmers, who are likely to lose some of their land through compulsory purchase, and then there's the politician who stands to gain his seat in parliament. There could also be a disgruntled member of staff out there or an angry boyfriend, who knows? So, we need to start eliminating as many of these suspects as quickly as possible. We need to interview all the farmers, including Johnston; we need to find out if they have an alibi for the time of death to eliminate them from the investigation. We need all of Donaldson's staff in Edinburgh to be interviewed—find out who has a grievance and what they did about it. We need to speak to the local Returning Officer and establish who will get Donaldson's seat in Parliament and then interview him or her. There will be a tonne of forensics to get through; some from the crime scene and others from Donaldson's home. So, plenty of work for us all."

Carter stood up and took over. "Thanks, Claire. Right, I think that sums up the enormity of our task. So tonight, I want the contents of Donaldson's briefcase examined. Look for anything unusual. Claire, that's your responsibility. Rambo, I want you to..."

Claire interrupted him. "Sorry, sir, can I just confirm that we have permission from the Chief Super to do that, keeping in mind what Munro said about confidential government papers?"

"You let me worry about that, Inspector. Now, Rambo, I want you to try and get into his laptop. I want to know the last thing he was looking at before he left the house and what time he turned it off."

"I'll do my best but government laptops are always encrypted, so it could take a while. It might be easier to wait until morning when I can get the code from their ICT security team."

Carter looked disappointed. "Well, do your best, we've not got a lot of time to spare. I've got the Chief Super breathing down my neck and she's got the Chief Constable on her case. Doyle and... sorry... what's your name, son?"

"DC Paul Black, sir."

"Right. Paul, I want you two to get in touch with all those other landowners on the list—find out if they have an alibi for the night of the murder. I'll deal with Johnston. Doyle, can you get onto forensics and find out when we can expect their findings? I want you to receive and record the evidence bags as they come back. Brian, try to get a hold of the Returning Officer for this area and set up a meeting. If he's the Chief Executive, he's bound to be listed on the civil emergency contact list."

Carter paused to consider if there was anything he had missed, but quickly decided that there was nothing more to add. "Okay then, that's enough to be getting on with for now. Let's get to it."

Chapter 18

Peter was parked outside Wallace's, office waiting for him to leave. It was now 6.26 p.m. and there was still no sign of him. Peter had arrived at 5.55 p.m., in time to see Wallace's staff leave at 6.00 p.m. but not Wallace. Peter was beginning to wonder if he had done the right thing when finally, the door opened and a man who Peter recognised to be Wallace appeared.

Wallace, a small-built man in his mid-fifties wearing a blue suit and carrying a brown leather briefcase, set the office alarm and locked the outer door before heading to his car. Peter noted Wallace had a black BMW similar to his own car and made up his mind to follow him.

Wallace pulled out onto the road and Peter duly followed him along Duke Street towards the town. At first, Peter thought Wallace was heading for the M8 motorway, but he soon realised he was heading towards the Great Western Road. After fifteen minutes, Wallace turned off the A82 at Kelvinbridge, took a few turns and pulled into the road leading to his modest sandstone home. Wallace slowed the BMW as it squeezed through the narrow gates of the tight driveway and then made his way carefully up towards his house.

Peter, being careful not to be noticed, drove on while taking note of the address. He checked his watch and decided it was time to make his way back home. He would come back and pay Wallace a visit when he had more time and hopefully would get the information he needed.

Chapter 19

Claire sat at her desk focussed on finding something of interest in the papers in Donaldson's briefcase. There were some draft reports on new wind farms which had been proposed and another providing an update on the controversial relief road. Munro had been correct; it was now being proposed that some land be purchased via Compulsory Purchase Order and that there was likely to be a legal challenge from James Johnston. According to the date on the draft report, the Committee was expected to meet in three weeks' time to determine the matter. Claire also noted that Donaldson had hand-written some comments on the draft report, and although his writing was poor, she could just about make out one of the questions which he had noted on the margin of page two: *'Does McLeish know?"* Claire took a mental note to find out who he was and his connection to the project. *Was he another one of the farmers affected by the CPO?* She would need to ask Munro.

Claire rubbed her eyes and stretched her arms out wide. She had been sitting there for just over two hours, and her joints were beginning to stiffen up. She got to her feet and slowly walked over to Carter's desk. She could see that some of the evidence bags from the crime scene had returned from forensics and were now being recorded and sorted on the table in the far corner of the room.

Carter looked up as she approached. "Oh, hi Claire, anything?"

"Not really. Just another name to check out, someone called McLeish. Donaldson had scribbled his name on the draft report on the relief road—probably another farmer. I'll check with Munro." She turned and looked at the evidence table. "That's going to take quite a while to sort through."

Carter nodded. "We should start to get the forensic reports in the morning."

"What about the pathologist?" she asked. "Have you heard anything further from the post-mortem?"

"Yes, I got a text a few minutes ago. He's sent blood and tissue samples to the lab for testing. He thinks Donaldson was poisoned."

"Poisoned!"

"Yeah, he reckons that something was used to stop his heart. We'll know for certain tomorrow but, at least we now know that it was murder."

Claire was not surprised at all. Everything that she had observed at the scene had suggested the same. "Have you told the Chief Super yet?" she asked.

"Yes. It's likely there will be a press conference in the morning, and we might even get a visit from the First Minister if we're lucky," he said sarcastically. "Apparently, Donaldson was a good friend of his."

"You're kidding? I didn't think Donaldson had any friends," said Claire, grinning.

"Well, it appears he has at least one, and unfortunately for us, that friend is going to demand quick results!"

"No surprise there! Anything else I can do tonight?" she asked, yawning. It had been a long day and she wasn't quite back to full power.

"Naw, you go home, I'll stay and make sure all the evidence is secured before we stop. I want you to go to the election office first thing in the morning—Brian has made an appointment with the Depute Returning Officer. Find out who is next in line to be elected and then arrange for them to come in, or we can go to them. I'll send Doyle and Armstrong to Edinburgh to interview Donaldson's staff. Rambo and Paul have arranged to see some of the other landowners affected by the road but I want us to interview Johnston in person. I'll get him to come in mid-morning after you've been to the election office. If he's not willing to come here to speak, then we'll see him. How's that sound?"

"Sounds like a plan!" said Claire.

"Good, now you go home and get plenty of rest. I need you to be at your best tomorrow."

"Will do, sir... and thanks."

Carter watched the young DI collect her coat and leave the office. He admired how well she was coping, given everything she had been through, and hoped she could keep it up. This investigation was going to be a tough one.

Chapter 20

On the way home, Claire remembered that she hadn't gotten back to Charlene. She took out her phone and made the call.

"Hello Claire," said Charlene.

"Hi Charlene, sorry to have taken so long to get back to you."

"Not a problem. I guess you've been busy with the Donaldson case."

"Yes, I take it you have seen the photo of me and the tree?"

"Yes, that was a bit unfortunate!" she chuckled.

"Yip. Anyway, how are you?"

"I'm fine," she replied quickly. "But more importantly, how are you?"

Claire paused to consider her response. "To be honest, I'm not great, but the distraction of the case is helping."

"Are you getting any help? Counselling?"

"Yes, and it has helped me a bit... with the loss of the baby. However, there's something else bothering me that I'd like to share with you, but I'm not going to be able to make it for lunch any time soon. It's about Peter."

"Oh, I see. Right, well, why don't we meet after work for a drink? I'm free tomorrow night. Just let me know when you expect to finish and I can come through to Dumbarton by train. Is there somewhere nice we can go?"

"There's the local hotel, the Abbotsford," suggested Claire.

"Is that the one just off the A82, before you reach the police station?"

"That's it. I could meet you at the train station at Dumbarton East, and we could walk up together. It's only about a fifteen-minute walk to the hotel."

"Sounds perfect," said Charlene. "Just give me a bit of notice when you're likely to finish and I'll let you know which train I'm on."

"I'm looking forward to it. See you tomorrow."

"Me too, bye Claire."

Claire put her phone away and continued walking home with a spring in her step. The fact that she now had someone to talk to openly and honestly about Peter was a welcome relief. Deep down inside her heart she hoped there was a way back for her and Peter, and perhaps Charlene would be able to help with that, but her head was sending her a different signal.

Chapter 21

For the first time in weeks, Claire woke up to the pleasant realisation that she had had a good night's sleep. She had been exhausted by the time she got home and after watching some rubbish TV documentary about water pollution, she had gone up to bed early and had slept all through the night. She felt great! Almost good enough to go for a run… almost, but she wasn't quite ready to face that particular hurdle. Not yet!

Peter had managed to stay up until after the ten o'clock news had finished before he finally went to bed. His night had been a bit less settled than Claire's, and so he decided to sleep on a little longer than usual. He had dreamt of confronting Wallace and beating a confession out of him, and then... he couldn't remember what happened after that. *Had he killed him*? His dream-filled thoughts were disturbed by Claire who announced that she was going to work. *Crap! What time is it?* He looked at the small digital clock on his bedside table which confirmed that it was 7.50 a.m. He sat up, stumbled out of bed and went straight into the shower. He would have time for a quick bite to eat before logging onto his work. Sally would just need to pee in the garden—he would walk her during his morning break.

~

Claire was the first to enter the incident room that morning. As usual, she started the day by opening her laptop and checking her emails. Carter had sent a message to say that he would be in a little later as the Chief Super had summoned him to brief the First Minister on progress before the press conference commenced.

Brian was next to arrive. "Morning, boss."

"Morning Brian. I'm just having a quick look at my emails, and then I'll be off to see the Depute Returning Officer. What's his name, again?"

"Matthew Andrews, he calls himself Matt. Seemed like a decent enough bloke on the phone. He's based down in the Municipal Buildings."

"What? The building where Peter and I were married?" queried Claire.

"The very same building. He says it's controlled entry during business hours, so you'll need to call him from the reception area when you get there. I've left the number on your desk."

It had been a long time since Claire had thought about their wedding day and now it only hurt her to think about it—she and Peter had been so happy together back then.

"Are you alright, boss?" asked Brian.

Claire hadn't realised that her eyes had filled up with tears. She quickly wiped them away and played down her emotions. "Just being a bit sentimental, you know what we women are like!" she joked.

Brian wasn't buying it but didn't want to push the point. "Do I ever!" he lied, and then sat down at his desk and turned on his laptop. "I'll make a start reviewing the forensics reports and give you an update when you get back from the Municipal Buildings."

Claire nodded and pretended to read her emails, but behind those crystal blue eyes, her mind was still reliving her wedding day—the happiest day of her life. She gave herself a shake and started thinking about work again. "Oh, by the way, Carter will be in later. He's having to meet the First Minister!"

Brian looked up from his laptop. "Nae luck! I canny stand politicians. It doesn't matter which party they represent – they're all the same. A bunch of useless …"

"Brian!" said Claire, feigning her shock that he was about to use such bad language. "Let's not stoop to the low levels of the MIT."

"You mean, DCI Carter," said Brian, smiling across the desk. "He's the worst of them all. Even worse than our DCI, and that's saying something."

"Yeah, he does tend to favour the use of certain expletives."

Brian smiled at Claire's careful use of language. "That's putting it *very* politely!" he goaded.

"Alright. Don't start all that nonsense about university again!"

"Well, you can't beat the University of Life. That's all the education you need."

"That's all the education *you* needed," responded Claire. "Anyway, enough of this nonsense, I'm off to see this Mr Andrews. I shouldn't be too long."

"Okay, boss. See you later."

Chapter 22

Doyle and Armstrong arrived in Edinburgh just after 9 a.m. and made their way through the tight security at the Scottish Government's building at Victoria Quay in Leith before being directed to the floor where Donaldson's staff were based.

They had made arrangements to interview each member of the team individually and had asked for a private room to be made available. They were shown to the small interview room and made themselves comfortable before the first member of Donaldson's team arrived.

Caroline Wilson, a middle-aged woman with sharp brown eyes and short brown hair tied back tight in a bun, entered the room and introduced herself as Mr Donaldson's Office Manager. She was wearing a plain white blouse with a black skirt and black shoes to match. Apart from some light blusher on her cheeks, it was difficult for Doyle to tell if she had any make-up on at all.

As had been agreed in the car journey to Leith, DC Jim Armstrong took the lead in the first interview and introduced himself and Doyle. They would alternate between each interview, each taking a turn to take notes while the other concentrated on the questions. Jim kicked off with the first question. "Mrs Wilson, how long did you work with Mr Donaldson?"

"Ever since he was first elected in… oh, now let me think! Yes, it must have been shortly after the 2011 Scottish Parliamentary Elections."

"So, is it fair to say that you knew him very well?" asked Jim.

"Yes, as well as anybody here, I suppose."

It was obvious to Jim that she was being a little guarded in her response. "I see, and during those years working with Mr. Donaldson, did he ever act inappropriately towards you?"

"No!" The response was quick and sharp.

"And what about other members of staff? Have there ever been any complaints about his behaviour?" asked Jim, this time maintaining eye contact with the woman.

Mrs Wilson looked less than comfortable and turned her head away from DC Armstrong. "What's this all about? I thought you were here to try and find out who killed the Minister… not to carry out a character assassination."

"That's exactly why we are here, Mrs Wilson. And, if it helps, we are trying to ascertain if anyone might hold a grudge against Mr Donaldson, so if you could answer the question, that would be helpful."

"I see. Okay… yes, there was one incident with a member of staff a few years ago, but nothing was ever proven. There was no actual investigation into her allegations and in the end she left on her own accord," she explained.

"What were the nature of the allegations?"

"I don't know the details but I think there may have been a suggestion that he touched her inappropriately."

Jim knew from her response that he wasn't going to get much more out of Mrs Wilson. She was doing her best to avoid saying anything bad about her ex-employer. "What was this employee's name?"

"Ruth McManus."

"Do you have an address or contact number for Ms McManus?"

"I don't, but some of the other girls might have her mobile number. They were friendly."

"Thank you, Mrs Wilson. May I ask, did *you* like Mr Donaldson?"

She hesitated before responding. "I'm sorry but I don't see the relevance of that question. He was my boss. I didn't need to like him or hate him. I just get on with my work."

Jim looked at Doyle, trying desperately to hide his frustration and then resumed eye contact with the woman. "Let me put the question another way—was Mr Donaldson popular with the staff?"

Mrs Wilson stared at the table. "No, I can't say that he was popular but that's not a reason for killing someone, is it? There are lots of unpopular people in this building, but none of them were found hanging from a tree, were they?"

Jim ignored the remark. "One final question, Mrs Wilson. Do you know anyone who would want to kill Mr Donaldson?"

"No, I don't," she said adamantly and stood up to leave.

Jim stood up and opened the door. "Can you ask Pen..., I mean Jenny Lane to come in next please?" Ever since he had read the name from the list, Jim could not get the Beatles' song out of his head.

"And could someone bring us a cup of tea?" asked Doyle.

The withering look on Mrs Wilson's face was enough to wipe the smile from his face. "There's a canteen on the ground floor," she said sourly. She turned and left the room.

Chapter 23

Claire entered the Municipal Buildings for the second time in her life. The first time was to get married by the local registrar. The hallway to the building was empty when she entered. She looked around, signed her name on the visitor book and then called the number she had been given.

"Election office," a male voice responded.

"Hi, I'm DI Claire Redding. I'm here to speak to Mr Andrews."

"I'll be right there," he said and hung up the phone. Within seconds, Andrews entered the hallway and introduced himself to the young detective. He was tall, of medium build and was wearing a well-worn grey suit, blue shirt and tie, which matched his greying beard and hair. He was exactly what Claire thought the Depute Returning Officer would look like—boring!

"Come on through. There's no one else in the office today. It's just me, so we can talk in private."

He led Claire into a short corridor with a photocopier and metal cabinet and then into the election office on the left. Claire stared at the wall of boxes on the far side of the room.

"That's all our election supplies and equipment," said Andrews, reading her mind. We're able to recycle most of the stuff that we use and this is the only place we can store it until the next election comes around. Please, take a seat," he said, pointing to the corner of the room with a round table and comfortable looking chairs with high backs.

"Can I get you a tea or a coffee?" he asked, staying on his feet, ready to fetch the drinks.

"No thanks, Mr Andrews. I'll not be long. I just need to know a few things about the election process now that Michael Donaldson is dead, and then I'll be on my way."

Andrews sat down. "Right. Yes, I read about that in the paper... hold on, you were the woman in the photograph, beside the tree."

Claire sighed. "Yes, that was me. I understand Mr Donaldson was a list MSP."

"Yes, that's correct. He was also a constituency candidate but was not elected in that particular contest," he explained. "I only met him very briefly at the count. Of course, he didn't know if he was going to be elected at that point, but given he was first on his party list, he was pretty much guaranteed a seat in the Parliament."

"Yes, so I was told; he was on the party list and I understand there doesn't need to be a by-election."

"Yes, that's correct, providing someone from the original list is still available to take his place."

This was new information to Claire. "Right, and can you tell me who that would be?"

"Oh, I'm not sure. I'll need to check with the Regional Returning Officer in Renfrew. They deal with the list candidates. We just send the constituency results over to them along with totals of the regional votes for this area, which they use to identify the successful candidates. They'll be able to tell me who the next unelected person on the party list was, but you'll need to confirm that they are still eligible."

"Eligible?" asked Claire.

"Yes, if they are still members of the political party that they stood for during the election and if they are still alive."

"Oh, I see." The thought that there may not be a successor had not even occurred to Claire.

"Give me a minute and I'll call Dave, over in Renfrew. I'm sure they will be looking into this already and might even have the answer to your question."

Claire sat patiently as Andrews took out his phone and speed-dialled his colleague over in Renfrewshire Council. He quickly explained what he was looking for, and Claire could tell from the smile on his face that he had been right; Renfrew had the answer. He thanked Dave for the information and hung up.

"Okay, so it appears that the next unelected person on the list was Councillor Daniel Hughes, and he's very much alive and is an active member of the party - he's currently serving as an elected member over in Paisley. You'll get his contact information on their website. I'm quite sure they have the same Committee Management Information System as us, so it should have all the councillor's public information, including contact details."

Claire stood up. "Thank you for your time, Mr Andrews. You have been extremely helpful."

"You're very welcome, Inspector."

Andrews escorted Claire to the exit. As she walked back to her car, she looked up to the windows of the Council Chamber where she and Peter had been married and felt a deep sadness descend on her, weighing her down, suppressing her inner happiness.

Chapter 24

Jenny Lane was quite different to Mrs Wilson. She wore a pink silk blouse, and a bright red pencil skirt which hugged her narrow hips so tightly that she could only take small scissor-like steps. The two-inch stiletto heels on her black patent leather shoes didn't help her mobility either. Doyle estimated that she could be anywhere between eighteen and twenty-four years old—it was difficult to tell given the amount of heavy make-up and fake tan that she was wearing. She smiled alluringly at the young detective as she sat down carefully on the seat opposite him.

Doyle's face reddened a little and he could feel the heat of his embarrassment rising above his collar. He managed to introduce himself and DC Armstrong without too much awkwardness and then moved on to the list of questions. "Miss Lane, how long have you been working with Mr Donaldson?"

"Please, call me Jenny," she said.

"Right... Jenny, so how long have you been working with Mr Donaldson?"

"Just over a year. I started here just after I finished university," she explained.

"And during that time, did he ever act inappropriately?"

"Well, let's just say he was a bit handy," she replied.

"Sorry, I'm not sure what you mean by *handy.*"

She rolled her eyes at Doyle. "I mean, he liked to use his hands." She raised her hands as if to reinforce the point.

"What? You mean, he groped you?" asked Doyle.

"Well, I wouldn't say he groped me. That suggests he was rough. No, he would pat my bottom occasionally or lean over me and press his groin against my thigh. You know, stuff like that."

"Right, and what about the other members of the team? Was he... *handy* with any of them?" asked Doyle.

"I'm not sure."

"What about Ruth McManus?"

"Who? Oh yes, I heard about her. She left before I started but I don't know anything about that. Never met her."

"Oh, I see," said Doyle, slightly disappointed. He paused and looked at the list of questions before continuing.

"Did you like Mr Donaldson?"

"He was alright, I suppose. A bit old for me," she replied. "I like my men a bit younger than that. How old are you, Detective?"

Doyle's face blushed. He wasn't sure how to respond to that question.

Thankfully, Jim stepped in to rescue him. "Miss Lane, do you know anyone who would want to hurt Mr Donaldson?"

"No, sorry."

"What about your boyfriend? How does he feel about Donaldson's inappropriate behaviour?"

She looked at Jim, "I don't have a boyfriend." She then turned slowly to Doyle and smiled, "I'm single!"

Chapter 25

James Johnston, a man in his late fifties, wearing a blue boiler suit, black boots and a grey woollen hat, was escorted by the Duty Sergeant to interview room two, up in the CID corridor. DCI Carter and DI Redding stood as he entered the room and introduced themselves. Claire estimated that Johnston must be at least six feet five inches tall. He looked fit and strong, his face was weather-beaten and his thick, long eyebrows looked as if they hadn't been trimmed in years, if at all. He sat down and removed his cap, revealing a balding head of short, reddish-brown hair. His scalp was pinkish white above the tan line running along the top of his forehead. It reminded Carter of the professional golfers who starred on the television—they would remove their golf caps at the eighteenth hole to reveal their pale white scalps, which looked weird in stark contrast to their well-tanned faces.

"Mr Johnston, I assume you know why you are here," said Carter.

"Aye, it's about Donaldson."

"That's correct. Did you know him?"

"No, I've never met the man."

"But, you know of him."

"Aye, you can say that again. I know who he is, or was - he's the bastard who wanted to buy my land and put a dirty big road right through the heart of my farm."

"So, you admit that you didn't like him?"

"Didn't like him? That's an understatement. I hated him and all those other government shits who want to buy my land for a song. Well, it's no goin' to happen. My lawyer is goin' to make sure of that."

Carter looked at Claire, signalling that it was her turn to take over the questioning. "Mr Johnston, I've read the government report on the relief road that makes it extremely clear that you and some other landowners were unhappy and upset by the plans. There was also mention of a Mr McLeish. Do you know him?"

"Sorry, I've no idea who he is."

"What about the other landowners affected by the road? Have you been in contact with any of them?"

"Not really, I got the impression that some of them were just holding out for more cash; they don't have as much to lose as me."

"Right. So, you can understand why some might think that you would have both the means and motive to have the MSP killed."

"Aye, I can see that. I'm no' stupid, hen. But given that you've not charged me with anything, and I'm not even under arrest, I assume you have absolutely no evidence whatsoever to suggest that I did it, which begs the question—when are you goin' to ask me the big question?"

Claire was taken aback by his blunt response but quickly recovered. "And what question would that be?"

"Did I kill Donaldson? And before you ask, no, I didn't. Is that it? Are we done here?"

"Not quite Mr Johnston," said Claire. "Where were you between midnight and 4 a.m.

on Monday, the time when Mr Donaldson was killed?"

Johnston grinned. "Home in bed with my wife, Fiona."

"And she will be able to confirm that?" asked Claire.

"Aye, of course she can. Now if there are no further questions, I'd like to go. I've got a farm to run."

"Not so fast, Mr Johnston," said Carter. He removed a few sheets of paper from the brown folder which he had in front of him. "I see from your police record that you have a history of violence. Would you mind telling us what happened back in 2002?"

"You're kidding? That was over twenty years ago."

"Maybe so, but it says here that you attacked another farmer in a local pub over a land dispute and pled guilty."

"Yes, but I was provoked. I was set up by that bastard, Brannigan. I bet it doesn't say that in your folder," said Johnston, pointing down at the table.

"So, what happened? Tell me, how were you provoked?"

Johnston sighed. He hadn't thought about Brannigan for a long time, and the memory of the incident in the pub still hurt him. "I was having a few pints at the end of an exhausting day. I was standing at the bar, minding my own business when Brannigan and one of his loud-mouthed pals came in. It was clear from the shouting and laughing that they had been elsewhere for a drink that night. Well, things only got worse when he spotted me. I should explain that a few weeks before the incident in the pub, I had bought his father's farm for what I considered to be a fair price. Unfortunately, the sale meant that Brannigan, who worked there all his life, was now out of a job. According to his father, he was a complete and utter useless waster and couldn't run a piss-up in a brewery, never mind a farm. His old man told me that he was happy to sell it to someone that he knew would look after the land and the animals properly."

"So, how did the fight start?" Carter prompted.

"Yes, so as I was saying, young Brannigan spots me at the bar and immediately comes over and starts accusing me of all sorts. I ignored him, but then he started poking me in the back, and then his diddy of a friend joined in... and I lose it. I turned and hit him square on the jaw, he went down like a ragdoll and banged his head on a table. He was knocked unconscious and someone called an ambulance. Then a couple of police officers come in and I'm under arrest and charged with assault."

Carter looked a bit puzzled. "If all that is true, why didn't you go to court and tell the truth? There must have been some witnesses there to back you up."

"I know, but I was not popular back then; I had bought up a few farms and well... let's just say there was a lot of jealousy goin' around. My solicitor advised me to plead guilty, so I ended up getting a non-custodial sentence. I had to serve 100 hours of community service, which was no easy task given that I was running one of the biggest farms in the area at the time. And let's face it, I was guilty. I punched him in the face when I should have walked away. Who knows what the court would have decided, but I couldn't risk it. I hope that answers your question. Am I free to go now?"

Carter knew that he had nothing solid to hold Johnston on, and after hearing his story, he felt a bit sorry for the man. "Yes, you're free to go. We'll check your alibi with Mrs Johnston and will be in touch if we have any further questions." Claire stood and escorted Johnston to the exit. When she returned to the CID corridor, Claire went straight into the incident room, where she knew Carter would be waiting for her.

"Well?" he asked, as she entered.

"Difficult to say. If he has a strong alibi, then it's probably not him."

Carter smiled at Claire. "Okay, so we move on. Let's get hold of that councillor over in Paisley and see what he's got to say for himself."

"No problem, I'll set it up, sir. I assume it's just the two of us again?"

"Yeah, and when we get back, I want the whole team in for a briefing. Let's hope Doyle and Armstrong are having better luck over in Edinburgh."

Claire looked around the office and could see that Brian was trying to get their attention. "What's up, Brian? Have you found something of interest in the forensic reports?"

Brian nodded. "I've got the report back from Donaldson's study and there's something not right about it. Normally, forensics would find evidence of fingerprints on the desk, glassware and other hard surfaces, but there was nothing."

"So, the killer must have cleaned up after themselves, which suggests that maybe Donaldson was taken from his study," said Carter.

"Or the room was cleaned by someone else before we got there," said Claire. "I remember thinking that the room was spotless when Brian and I looked it over."

Carter and Brian looked confused.

"Someone else?" asked Carter. "You mean an accomplice?"

"Well, not necessarily. The Donaldsons have a gardener to take care of the grounds, so it wouldn't surprise me if they also had a cleaner to take care of the house. We need to check if there is a cleaner and when she's scheduled to do the cleaning."

"I'll call Jenny and find out," Brian offered.

"Hold on a minute. Let's think this through a bit more," said Carter. "Let's assume the room was cleaned by the killer. If Mr Donaldson was taken from the room, surely there would have been a struggle, some noise, and Mrs Donaldson would have heard something?"

Claire was not convinced. "I'm not sure. It's a big house, and if she were in a deep sleep at the time when her husband was taken, then it's most likely she wouldn't have heard anything at all."

Brian nodded in agreement. "Agnes says that you could walk a herd of elephants through my room when I was sleeping and I wouldn't hear a thing."

"Okay, let's assume that she couldn't hear anything then. Why wasn't there any sign of a struggle? Damaged furniture, broken glasses. He wouldn't just get up and leave peacefully," argued Carter.

"He would if he had a gun pointing at him," said Claire.

"Good point," said Carter pointing his fingers at Claire as if he were holding a gun. "Okay, Brian, find out about the cleaner and we can discuss further when Claire and I get back from Paisley."

"Paisley," said Brian curiously.

Claire explained, "Yes, that's where Donaldson's political successor is based. We should only be an hour or so. I don't suppose there's been any sign of the pathology report yet. It would be good to know the actual cause of death."

"No, but I'll contact you as soon as we hear anything?" said Brian.

"Right then, we're off to Paisley," said Carter.

Chapter 26

Located on the south side of the River Clyde, approximately twenty minutes from Dumbarton by car, Paisley was the main town in Renfrewshire. It was home to the Sheriff Court and the headquarters of Renfrewshire Council, a bit like Dumbarton, but with a bigger population.

Carter and Claire climbed the steep set of stairs leading up to the main reception area of Renfrewshire Council's headquarters and then waited for Councillor Danny Hughes to meet them. After some brief introductions, he took them to a small interview room, away from the noise of the busy reception area. Claire noted the area was also used by the Registration Service and that members of the public were being issued with a ticket and a number on arrival, just like the collection system in Argos. It was a far cry from the quiet, peaceful setting of the registration office in Dumbarton.

Councillor Hughes looked to be in his early forties, with jet-black, greasy hair combed into a side-parting. His hazel eyes were magnified by his spectacles which made them look over-sized, like those of a Looney Tunes character. He wore a white shirt with the top button open and grey slacks with a black belt. His large beer belly stretched the bottom of the thin cotton shirt to its limits and Claire was certain that the buttons were about to explode if any further pressure was applied.

They all sat down around a small white cylindrical table.

Carter took the lead and got right to the point. "Councillor Hughes, I'm sure you will have heard that Michael Donaldson, MSP, has been found hanged."

"Yes, of course, it was terrible news."

"Terrible, yes, but I understand that you will gain his seat in Parliament"

"Yes, so I have been told but I... wait a minute. You don't think that I had anything to do with his death, do you? Is that why you are here?"

"Yes, but please understand that we need to eliminate all possibilities. This is now a murder investigation so we are speaking to anyone who might have had a motive to kill him."

Hughes looked perturbed. "Murder! Someone killed him! Right, okay I can see why you need to speak to me but I had nothing to do with it. I barely knew the man."

"Have you met him, in person?" asked Claire.

He nodded. "Yes, but only at our party events, you know, the annual conference and things like that. I didn't know him on a personal level."

"When was the last time you saw him?" asked Carter.

"Oh, I couldn't say off-hand. Let me think. There was the annual conference in October and the Christmas Party in December and… no, that was it. Yes, it was December, I can get you the actual date if that helps?"

"No, that won't be necessary, thanks," said Carter.

Carter and Claire looked at each other disappointingly. Both knew there was little to go on so it was time for the final question, which Carter would ask. "One final question,

Councillor Hughes. Where were you between the hours of midnight and 4 a.m. on Monday, the night Mr Donaldson was killed?"

For the first time, Councillor Hughes hesitated. "I, eh, emm, spent the night in a hotel. I was at an event in Perth."

"And were you alone in the hotel room?" asked Claire, sensing the councillor's newfound anxiety—sweat appeared on his brow as his face reddened.

Hughes wiped it off with the sleeve of his shirt, leaving a greasy stain. "Well, yes and no," he replied.

"What does that mean?" asked Claire.

"I was with someone for part of the night and then they left."

Claire nodded, knowingly. She looked at his hands, which were now clasped tightly on the table and noticed the wedding band. "I see. Are you married, Councillor Hughes?"

"Yes."

"And is it fair to assume that you were not with your wife that night?"

Again, he hesitated, trying carefully to find the right words. "Yes, I was with another woman."

"I'm afraid you will need to tell us her name as we will need to check out your alibi."

Hughes's face was now the colour of ripe beetroot. "I can't. She's married. It'll…"

"Mr Hughes, I can assure you that we will act with the utmost sensitivity and in complete confidence. We have no interest in your affair, we just need to know that you were in the hotel room during those hours so we can eliminate you from our list of suspects."

Hughes sat there in silence, contemplating what to do. If news of his affair got out, he would probably be removed from the party list and lose his seat in Parliament.

Carter read his mind and added further fuel to the fire that was burning inside the bedraggled councillor. "Mr Hughes, I should also warn you that it is an offence to withhold any information which is relevant to our investigation and therefore failure to disclose your alibi could lead to your arrest." Carter knew that he was stretching it a bit with that statement and would never make such a threat in front of a solicitor, but Hughes didn't know that.

"You promise to keep it confidential. No one else needs to know?"

Claire smiled. "Yes, so who did you spend the night with?"

Chapter 27

Doyle and Armstrong had finished interviewing all of Donaldson's staff and were driving back down the M8, towards Glasgow. The last two interviews had confirmed what they had already established—Donaldson was an unpopular creep, who had a fondness for younger women and had been extremely lucky that no formal complaint had been made against him.

The two detectives had managed to get a contact number for Ruth McManus and had arranged to interview her at her home in Livingstone, which just happened to be on the route back to Dumbarton. Ruth was now working for West Lothian Council as an administrative assistant and was currently working from home, as were most back-office admin staff.

When she answered the door, she was dressed casually, wearing blue jeans, a green sweater and large pink slippers on her feet. Both policemen noticed that she was both young and attractive—a combination which they now knew brought out the worst in Donaldson. After brief introductions, Ruth invited the two men into her small one-bedroom flat.

"Ms McManus, is it okay if I call you Ruth?" asked DC Jim Armstrong, breaking the ice.

She smiled and nodded. "Yes, Ruth is fine."

Jim continued. "Thank you, Ruth. As we explained earlier, we are investigating the death of Michael Donaldson, MSP. I understand you used to work for him. Is that correct?"

"Yes… yes, I did, but that was a wee while ago," she replied hesitantly.

Jim could see the concern on her face and decided to get straight to the point. "And I also understand there was an incident between you and Mr Donaldson that resulted in you leaving the job. Is that correct?"

Ruth smiled. She now understood where this conversation was heading. "Yes, that's correct. Who have you been talking to? That old witch, Wilson?"

Jim didn't respond to the comment. "Can you tell us what happened?" he asked.

"Okay, so Mike, I mean Mr Donaldson, was well-known in the office for being a bit careless with his hands—some of the girls liked the attention but I wasn't one of them. It all started innocently with the occasional accidental contact, brushing by each other in the corridor or he would lean over the desk, pretending to reach for a folder and put his arm around you—nothing serious. But one thing led to another and he started to get a bit braver. You know, testing what he could get away with. I got fed up with it and told him off and it was fine. He behaved himself for a while, but it was at the office Christmas party when things got out of hand—we were all drinking and having a laugh when he turned up and joined in the festivities and... Sorry." She paused as the upsetting memory of the incident came back to her.

"Do you need a minute?" asked Jim.

"No, I'll be fine. It's just been a while since I had to think about it."

Jim nodded sympathetically. "Take your time, there's no rush."

Ruth nodded back, "I'll just get some water if that's okay? Would you like anything to drink?"

Before Jim could decline, Doyle jumped in. "A cup of tea would be great. It's a long journey back to Dumbarton."

Ruth looked to Jim, who nodded. "Yes, I may as well. Thank you."

Ruth stood up and headed for the kitchen.

"Dirty bastard!" whispered Doyle to his colleague. "Feeling up all these young girls and getting away with it just because he was a big knob politician. Well, I'm glad he's dead."

"Yeah, but remember, we have a job to do here. It doesn't matter if we like the man or not. Our focus is on catching his killer."

"Aye, I know but it's clear that Ruth didn't do it," said Doyle.

"And how would you know that? We don't know where she was on the night of the murder and whether or not she has an alibi."

"Aye, okay, but she's doing a grand job of providing us with a motive. She wouldn't do that if she were guilty."

Just at that moment, Ruth walked into the room with a tray of drinks. "Guilty? Do you think that I killed him? Do I need a lawyer?"

If looks could kill, Doyle was a dead man.

"No, not at all," said Jim, giving Doyle another dirty look. She looked at Doyle, who nodded and back to Jim, who smiled. "Honestly, we have no reason to believe that you did anything wrong."

This appeared to reassure her and she sat down and handed out the cups of tea. The two men helped themselves to milk and sugar and biscuits before resuming the questioning. Jim gobbled down a digestive, sipped some more tea and then cleared his throat before speaking. "You were going to tell us about the incident at the office party."

"Oh yes, so I was," she said hesitantly. She gave out a long sigh and then told the two men the whole sordid story. "It was getting on a bit and we all had been drinking and dancing to the music. Everyone was having an enjoyable time. I got up and went to the loo, which was at the other end of the corridor from where the party was happening. I entered the toilets, turned and saw that Mike had followed me into the ladies. At first, I thought he had made a mistake and pointed out to him that the gents was next door. He just laughed as if I was telling a joke or something and then he started to tell me how much he fancied me, that it was driving him crazy and that he wanted to have me, right there and then, in the bloody toilet! I told him to get lost, that I wasn't interested and tried to leave, but he blocked the door and grabbed me, pulling me towards him. He put his hand between my legs and tried to pull my pants down. I was raging and kneed him in the balls. He fell to the ground holding his groin, looking at me as if I was off my head. Anyway, I managed to squeeze by him, opened the door and made my way back to the party."

"And did you report this to anyone?" asked Jim.

"Not that night, I just grabbed my coat and bag and went home. When I returned to work, I told Mrs Wilson all about the incident and that I wanted to make a formal complaint."

"And what happened?"

"She told me that it was my word against his and that I should let it drop if I knew what was good for me. I told her that I wasn't happy with that and she suggested that perhaps I should leave the job. I was raging and decided that I wasn't going anywhere. Why should I? He was at fault, not me!" she exclaimed.

Jim and Doyle glanced at each other. This was a very different version of the story first told by Mrs Wilson.

"But you did leave, so what happened?" asked Jim.

"Nothing happened. I told myself I could put up with him, but I couldn't. Every time he came into the office he made my skin crawl. So I found myself another job and surprise, surprise, Mrs Wilson gave me a glowing reference."

"I see," said Jim. "Did you have a boyfriend at the time?"

"Yeah, I did. But what's that got to do with this?"

"Did your boyfriend know about Donaldson's behaviour and why you left the job?"

"Yes, I told him all about it."

"And how did he react? Was he angry?" asked Doyle.

"Oh, I see where this is going. You want to know if Craig could have killed Donaldson. Is that it?"

Jim cut in before Doyle could respond. "We're trying to eliminate anyone who might have had a motive to kill Mr Donaldson, so it would be helpful to know if... Craig, was it?"

She nodded, "Craig Thomson."

"Right. Did Craig hold a grudge against Donaldson?" asked Jim.

Ruth shook her head. "Craig and I split up shortly after I changed jobs. He was angry at the time and made a few threats to go and see Donaldson, but in the end, he didn't do anything and it all fizzled out."

"Why did you break up?" asked Doyle.

"Craig found someone else—or rather I found Craig in bed with someone else," she said bitterly.

"And what about you? Are you on your own now?" asked Jim.

"No, I've met someone else. James Jack."

"And does James know about Donaldson?"

"No, why would he? I had no reason to burden James with my baggage, and as I said... it was over. I had left the job by the time James and I had met, so there was no need."

Jim nodded. "Fair enough. That leaves me with one last question. Where were you between the hours of 12 midnight and 4 a.m. on Monday, the night when Michael Donaldson was killed?"

Ruth looked upset that Jim had even felt the need to ask the question but knew she had to provide an answer. "I was at home, in bed with James."

"And he will be able to confirm this?" asked Doyle.

"Yes."

"Great, if you can give us the contact numbers for both James and Craig, that would be most helpful," Jim responded.

Ruth gave the information to Doyle and the two men left the flat disappointed that they were no closer to catching the killer—almost everyone they had spoken with had good reason to dislike or even hate Donaldson, but none had given any indication that they, or their boyfriends, had sufficient motive to kill him. It was going to be a long journey back to Dumbarton.

Chapter 28

The full team were back in the incident room waiting for Carter to start the briefing. Carter was waiting anxiously for the Chief Superintendent to arrive; she had asked to sit in on the briefing and was running a little late. Again, Carter had asked Claire to share the briefing and so she was ready to do her bit, albeit a little nervous. She had delivered numerous briefings before but this would be her first in the presence of the Chief Superintendent.

The buzz in the room turned to silence when Chief Superintendent Ralston entered. She looked around and then stood at the back and nodded to Carter, indicating that he could proceed.

"Okay folks, we've got a lot to get through so let's get started." Carter walked over to the incident board and pointed to the name at the top of the board. "David Donaldson has openly admitted that he hated his brother, Michael Donaldson. He accused him of stealing his share of the inheritance and of being a hypocritical homophobe." Carter could see the confused look on some of the faces in the room. "David is gay and claims that Michael was disgusted when he found out that he was a homosexual, despite having voted for Same Sex Marriage. According to David, Michael's homophobia was the reason why he did not invite David to his wedding." Carter paused to allow that piece of information to be absorbed and then continued. "David Donaldson does not have an alibi for the night of his brother's death; he was home alone, so we can't rule him out, but both DI Redding and I felt that he was being completely honest with us and if he wasn't his performance deserved to win a bloody OSCAR!"

A few murmurs of laughter could be heard around the room.

"DCI Carter," said Ralston, raising her hand slightly to get his attention. "Just to be clear. Are we saying that David Donaldson is still a person of interest?"

"Yes, ma'am. We have no evidence to suggest that he did it but we believe he had the strongest motive. His motive also fits with the notion of betrayal as suggested by the 30 pieces of silver found below the tree. The Judas Tree!"

Ralston nodded and indicated that he should continue.

"Our next person of interest is James Johnston—a farmer who stands to lose his land and who also admits to hating Donaldson. However, he claims he has never met Donaldson. However, Johnston, who has a history of violence, has an alibi which has been confirmed by his wife—he was home in bed. Claire, do you want to take over from here?"

Claire stood and walked over to the incident board. "Thank you, sir." She took a breath, took a quick look at the board and steadied herself before speaking. "We also looked at the possibility of there being a political motive for the killing. Who would benefit from Donaldson's death? This part of the investigation led us to Councillor Daniel Hughes in Paisley who has provided an alibi which has yet to be confirmed. He claims to have spent the night with Mrs Caroline Wilson. He has provided her mobile telephone number and…"

Jim Armstrong stood up. "Sorry, but did you say that he was sleeping with Caroline Wilson?"

"Yes, why?" asked Claire, a little put out that Jim had interrupted her flow.

"Because Donaldson's Office Manager is also called Caroline Wilson," he replied. "And what's more, Doyle and I suspect that she may have tried to mislead us when interviewed."

"She tried to mislead you?" asked Claire, now extremely interested in what Jim had to say.

"Yes, when we asked her about the accusation that Donaldson had behaved inappropriately towards some members of staff, and by that I mean sexual harassment, she totally played it down. According to Ruth McManus, the former employee who left because of Donaldson's behaviour, Caroline Wilson refused to do anything about her complaint against Donaldson."

"That is interesting. Of course, it could be a coincidence—it could be another Caroline Wilson."

Carter interrupted her. "I don't believe in coincidence Inspector, do you?"

Claire smiled at Carter. She knew he was referring to their previous case. "No, sir, I don't, so let's follow up on that after the briefing."

Jim nodded, satisfied that he had already made a valuable contribution to the briefing.

"Claire, remind me. How did we find out about Donaldson's so called inappropriate behaviour?" asked Ralston.

"Of course, ma'am. His Parliamentary Assistant, Malcom Munro, mentioned it when interviewed. This prompted DCI Carter to send DC Armstrong and DC Doyle to interview his staff."

"Right, so as long as we have no evidence to suggest that his... bad behaviour was connected to his death, I think we all need to be very careful what we say out there and ensure that there are no leaks."

Doyle suddenly felt uncomfortable. He had been removed from the previous MIT case in Dumbarton for accidentally leaking information. Claire looked around the room but did not focus on Doyle, whom she knew would be feeling the heat. "I'm sure we are all aware that what is shared in this room, stays in this room, ma'am."

Ralston nodded her approval and Claire took that as signal to continue. "So, as I was saying we will need to follow up on the connection between Caroline Wilson and Councillor Daniel Hughes."

This time, Claire was interrupted by Doyle, who was now keen to contribute. "We also need to interview Ruth McManus's ex-boyfriend, Craig Thomson, as he had knowledge of Donaldson's behaviour towards Ruth and might hold a grudge. It's a long shot but let's find him and eliminate him from our enquiries."

"Yes, let's leave no stone unturned," said Claire smiling and looked at Carter to confirm that she was finished with her part of the briefing. He stood and approached the board. "Right, now onto other matters. Rambo, have you managed to get into Donaldson's laptop?"

Rambo stood up and looked around the room nervously before speaking. "Yes boss, it took a while but I managed to get hold of the right person in the Scottish Government IT department and now have the encryption code and password. You asked me to check the last email sent by Donaldson. I did, and it was addressed to *s dot mcleish 101 at busmail dot co dot UK.*"

Claire and Carter looked at each other and nodded. This tied in with the note on the report on the new road that Claire found in Donaldson's case '*Does McLeish know?*'

"What did the message say?" asked Carter eager to connect the dots.

Rambo picked up his pad in order to give the exact wording. "Can we meet ASAP?"

"Is that it?" snapped Carter, clearly disappointed.

"What time was the message sent?" asked Claire, getting to her feet.

"Eleven thirty-six," replied Rambo.

"Did McLeish reply to the message?" she asked.

"No, I did check and there was nothing in Donaldson's inbox."

Carter cut in again before Claire could continue. "What about his phone? Have you managed to access his text messages?"

"Yes, but I didn't know I was looking for a message from McLeish, so I'll check again."

Carter approached the board and added McLeish's name in bold print. "Okay, good, let's find out who he is and get him in for questioning. It may be nothing but it could be something."

Rambo nodded obediently.

Claire was back on her feet. "Sir, I find it strange that Donaldson's PA, Malcolm Munro didn't know Mcleish. You would have thought that if he was connected to the new road project then Munro would know him."

Carter nodded pensively. "Yeah, which is another good reason why we need to find out who he is."

"I should be able to use his email address to identify him," offered Rambo. "Might take a bit of time though."

"Or we could simply email the man and see if he responds," said Claire.

Rambo looked slightly embarrassed. "Yes, we could try that first."

"Good, go ahead," said Carter. "Okay, forensics. Brian—tell everybody about your findings so far." He looked up and saw the Chief Super look at her watch. She indicated to Carter that she had to go and he nodded back as she made her way out of the room.

Brian shared his news about the study being cleaned but kept his latest news to last. "...so I contacted Jenny Barnes to find out if the Donaldson's have a cleaner and it turns out they do. Deirdre Muldoon—she usually cleans every Friday but it so happens that she had to attend a family funeral last Friday and so came in early on Monday morning to clean the house. I contacted her to double check and she confirmed this was the case. She also confirmed that she cleaned the ground floor first as Mrs Donaldson was still in her bed when she got in at 6 a.m., so she would have cleaned the study before we searched it."

"She must be a bloody good cleaner!" Carter interjected. "The forensic team found nothing."

"It does sound a bit suspicious, sir," said Brian.

Carter looked at Claire and she guessed what he was thinking. "Might be worth paying another visit to Mrs Donaldson," he suggested.

Before Claire could respond, DC Paul Black cut in. "Sir, you asked me to look into the question of inheritance and insurance. Would this be a suitable time to share my findings?"

"As good a time as any... Paul, isn't it?" said Carter.

"Yes, sir," said Paul, who was visibly pleased that Carter had finally remembered his name. "So, as we thought, Mrs Donaldson will inherit everything, the property and its contents, vehicles, cash in bank and she is the sole named beneficiary on Michael Donaldson's insurance policy which will pay out the sum of two million pounds."

There was a sharp intake of breath around the room.

"Right, well I think that counts as a pretty good motive for murder. Claire—I think it's time we take a closer look at Mrs Carly Donaldson."

"Yes, sir, but we're going to have to be very careful."

"Careful is my middle-name, Claire," said Carter. "Right, let's get to it."

~

Peter was sitting at his laptop at home staring at the screen. He had decided to do some more research into Wallace before he paid him a visit. According to the electoral roll, Wallace was the sole occupant of the house in Kelvinbridge. However, Peter didn't want to rely purely on this and after some searching, he eventually found what he was looking for—confirmation that Wallace was divorced and had no dependants. It was therefore likely that Wallace was living alone, unless of course he had a partner who hadn't registered with Electoral Registration Office.

Peter decided he would take a chance. Claire had told him she was going out with a friend later that night which would give him the perfect opportunity to see Wallace without her realising he was gone. All he had to do now was work a way to make Wallace talk.

Chapter 29

Carter and Claire were sitting in the incident room discussing how they were going to deal with Mrs Donaldson. It was clear that they both had different ideas about how to approach it. Unlike Carter, Claire was reluctant to confront the woman face-on; they still had no evidence against her and although a financial motive had now been firmly established, she believed that it was not enough to bring Mrs Donaldson in for questioning.

Carter listened to Claire's argument and then conceded. "Okay, so what do you suggest that we do?"

"Well, if Mrs Donaldson was involved in her husband's death, she must have had some help. She couldn't lift his body and hang it from the tree on her own. She's just not strong enough."

"So, you're thinking that she might have a lover who helped her," Carter mused.

"Yes, so let's interview the cleaner and the gardener and find out who she's been seeing recently. You never know, perhaps one of them will have seen or overheard something important."

Carter considered this and nodded. "Okay, we'll do it your way for now, but if we uncover any hard evidence, I want her in."

Claire smiled. "Brian's going through the rest of the forensics from the scene of the crime. Maybe there's something there that will help."

"Maybe, but..." Carter was interrupted by the ring of his mobile phone. He checked to see who the call was from before answering and whispered to Claire. "It's McAlpine."

Carter swiped the green arrow to accept the call and immediately put it on speaker so Claire could hear the conversation. "Hello Dr McAlpine. What do you have for me?"

"Hello, Chief Inspector. I've received the lab reports and have some interesting findings to report," replied McAlpine, who then paused for dramatic effect.

"Well, don't keep me waiting. What is it?" snapped Carter.

"It turns out that I was right—our distinguished MSP was poisoned before he died."

"Right. What kind of poison?" asked Carter.

"That's what is so interesting about this case. We found traces of a substance called viscumin in his bloodstream and digestive system."

"Viscumin?" asked Carter. He looked up at Claire, who looked just as puzzled as he did.

"Yes, it's found in mistletoe and is very similar to ricin."

"Ricin!" Carter exclaimed. "Bloody hell, don't tell me the Russians are involved!"

"I said it was *similar* to ricin," he said, correcting Carter. "It works the same way as the toxic chemicals in ricin, but its origin is very different—Viscum Album, otherwise known as European Mistletoe, is very common in these parts."

"So, anyone with access to mistletoe could have poisoned him?" asked Carter.

"Well, not really. You see, in order to extract the highly toxic viscumin from the plant, you would need to have a good knowledge of plants and most likely have some knowledge of biochemistry."

"Right, well that should narrow down our list of suspects," said Carter.

"Glad to be of help," said McAlpine. "I'll send the full toxicology report over to you in a few minutes."

"Thank you," replied Carter and hung up the call. He looked at Claire. "Any thoughts?"

"Lots. Okay, so we now know he was poisoned, which helps to explain how the killer managed to get him out of the house without any fuss or noise."

"Right, so we need to establish how the killer poisoned him?"

"Yes, traces were found in his bloodstream and digestive system so presumably they hid it in his food or drink?"

Carter nodded. "So that suggests it was someone who he knew or trusted."

"Which brings us back to his wife. She had both motive and opportunity to poison him," said Claire.

"Yes, but I doubt that she has the knowledge to produce the viscumin. I've never even heard of it before. Have you?"

Carter shook his head. "Nope, this is a first for me. It would be very convenient if Mrs Donaldson had studied biochemistry at university."

Claire smiled. "Very convenient, so we need to look into that. Shouldn't be too difficult."

"We could ask the family liaison officer. What was her name again?" asked Carter.

"Jenny, Jenny Barnes," Claire replied. "Or we could bring her in for questioning, as you suggested earlier."

Carter shook his head. "No, I think you were right. Also, it would be impossible to question her again without letting on that we were onto her, and that could be counterproductive. No, let's speak to the cleaner and gardener first and see if anyone has been seeing Mrs Donaldson. Maybe someone that has a background in biochemistry?"

Claire thought back to the study and the whisky decanter. "If she did poison him in the house then she did a decent job of getting rid of the evidence, the forensic team found nothing in the study. I'll get Brian to check that they tested the contents of the decanter."

"They better have or there'll be trouble," growled Carter.

"Even if they did, my gut says there'll be no trace left of the poison."

Carter nodded. "You're probably right, but worth checking all the same."

Chapter 30

Malcolm Munro was sitting at his desk in Victoria Quay, staring out the window at the murky water of the unused Victoria Dock. The last couple of days had been tumultuous following the unexpected death of the government minister, and now the uncertainty over Donaldson's replacement was bearing down heavily on the troubled civil servant. He had worked closely with Donaldson over the past two years and consequently, both men had formed a clear understanding of what they wanted to achieve and how they wanted to achieve it. The new road project in West Dunbartonshire had been a major priority for his department and there were several interested parties with a vested interest in its success. None more so than Clelland McLeish, owner of the biggest construction company in Scotland. Munro regretted lying to the police about knowing McLeish but felt he had no choice. If the police were to find out that McLeish's company was receiving inside information on the project, then Munro's career would be over and Donaldson's reputation would be in tatters. Munro was also convinced that McLeish had nothing to do with Donaldson's death. Why would he? After all, McLeish had Donaldson in his back pocket, thanks to Munro's efforts. Unless, of course, Donaldson was having second thoughts. But if he had, he had hidden them well from Munro. His thought pattern was disturbed by the ringing tone of his mobile phone. He looked at the screen and took a large intake of air before answering the call that he had been expecting. It was McLeish.

"Hello, Clelland. How are you?"

"Cut the crap Munro and tell me what's going on," snarled McLeish.

"I'm still waiting to hear about Donaldson's replacement if that's what you mean."

"Of course, that's what I mean. I need to know who is going to get the job and if they are on board with the new road. I've invested a lot of time and money into this project, and I had better not be disappointed."

"Look, Clelland, I'll let you know as soon as I hear anything, but everything is under control. Even if they do appoint someone else, it'll take some time for that person to get to grips with the project. And what's more, the depute chair of the Committee, who is currently in charge of things, is totally behind the project as it stands so it's just a matter of time before the proposal gets the final go-ahead." Munro spoke with more confidence than he felt, but it was important to keep McLeish at bay. "Clelland... I think we should keep our communication to a minimum over the next few days."

"And why is that?" asked McLeish.

"Because the police asked me if I knew anyone called McLeish. I denied it, of course..."

"How did they get my name?" Mcleish asked. There was a coldness to his voice which scared Munro a little.

"Apparently, Mike had scribbled your name on the copy of the draft report, which they found in his briefcase."

Munro held his phone away from his ear as Mcleish yelled a barrage of expletives down the line and then there was a silence, which Munro decided to fill. "Clelland! Calm down.

They're investigating a murder; they're not interested in the road project, or you for that matter. It looks to me that they are just clutching at straws—they don't know who you are, so it's going to be fine."

"Is that so? If they don't know who I am, then why am I getting emails from a Sergeant Bahanda in Dumbarton? It all makes sense now!"

The colour drained from Munro's face and then the penny dropped. "His laptop! They must have access to his emails."

Munro's remarks were followed by another barrage of McLeish's favourite expletives. Munro took another gulp of air before speaking; his heart was now racing. "What are you going to do about it?"

"What do you think? I'm going to have to meet them, otherwise, it'll look even more suspicious."

"You can't tell them that you know me. I've already denied…"

"Relax, I'm not that stupid. If they ask about the road report, I'll just say that Donaldson and I were old friends and that I have no idea why he would want to talk to me about it and suggest that perhaps he was looking for some advice, given my background. And when they ask about his death then all I need to do is think up an alibi for the night of his death."

"What do you mean *think up an alibi*? You didn't…" The line went dead.

Chapter 31

"Boss, do you have a minute?" asked Brian, as he approached Claire's desk.

"Sure, what's up? Take a seat."

Brian sat down opposite Claire. He had a printed copy of the forensic report on the crime scene at the Judas Tree in his hand. "Thanks. I've finished looking over the forensic report and thought I should give you the heads up on a few details."

"Sounds interesting, go on."

"Right. So firstly, all the coins had been wiped clean. Forensics found nothing."

"Which means they were put there by the killer and didn't accidentally fall out of Donaldson's pockets when he was strung up."

"Exactly, so it appears that the choice of the tree and the use of coins is the killer's way of letting us know that he was betrayed in some way by Donaldson."

Claire nodded. "Yip, it certainly looks that way. It's either that or a huge red herring. Anything else?"

"Yeah, they found traces of soft brown leather on the rope."

"So, the killer was wearing gloves." Claire pondered.

"Forensics are trying to see if they can match the leather to a particular product but it may not be possible."

"Hmm, okay. Well, we'll just need to wait and see what they discover. Anything else?"

Brian nodded and grinned. He had kept the best for last. "The SOCO also found tyre marks behind the tree."

"Behind the tree?" asked Claire. "Do you mean further down the hill?"

"Yes!"

Claire knew what Brian was getting at. "Right, so the killer could have attached the rope to the vehicle to haul Donaldson's body up the tree, which ties in neatly with the pathologist's findings. Hold on, we struggled to get our four-by-fours along that path. How on earth did the killer... wait, do forensics think it was a tractor?"

Brian was ready to burst with excitement. "Yes! They have measured the distance between the wheels and have taken plaster casts of the tyre pattern, and will try to match them to a specific make or model. They are quite hopeful that they can—it's only a matter of time."

"That's great, Brian. I'd better share this with Carter as soon as he returns."

Brian looked round the room. "Where is he?"

"In Glasgow, his MIT boss called him in to discuss another case his team are dealing with. He was raging."

"I can imagine," said Brian.

"What about you? What's next?"

"Interviewing Donaldson's cleaner and gardener, but I can't get hold of either of them on the numbers that Jenny gave me."

"They probably don't respond to telephone numbers that they don't recognise. I don't either – it's usually timeshare or some other sales call."

Claire nodded resignedly. "Or they're still working and haven't checked their phones. I've left a message for both to call me back."

Claire looked beyond Brian where she could see Rambo lurking in the background. "Rambo! What's up?"

"I've just had a response from Mr McLeish. He's agreed to see us tomorrow morning. He's asked if we could make it 8.30 a.m., to fit with his work schedule."

"That should be fine. Go ahead and confirm with him. DCI Carter and I will see him after the morning briefing. Oh, and can you book an interview room for us? Thanks, Rambo."

"No problem, boss."

Brian turned to Claire and smiled. "Boss! Looks like you're finally beginning to make an impression on our friends from the MIT."

"About bloomin' time!" Claire joked. "Right, give me that report. I want to see what else they've found."

"Leave no stone unturned, boss," Brian sniggered.

"Don't you start!" she laughed. "On a more serious note, I want you to review all the statements and interview notes taken so far—see if there are any questions left unanswered. There's so much of it now, it would be easy to overlook something important."

"Sure thing, boss. No stone un…"

"Brian!"

The big man turned away laughing. He loved winding Claire up. It made his day.

Chapter 32

Claire finished putting on her lipstick in the mirror in the hall and then buttoned up her coat, ready to go and meet Charlene at the train station at Dumbarton East. It was only a few minutes' walk from her home in Silverton Avenue.

Peter was busy in the kitchen clearing away his dinner dishes as Claire had decided to eat at the hotel and had booked a table in the main restaurant on her way home from the station. She was excited at the prospect of seeing Charlene again. Charlene, a professor of Psychiatry at Glasgow University, had assisted Claire when hunting down a serial killer, and since then, they had become friends.

"That's me away," said Claire, popping her head around the kitchen door.

Peter turned and smiled. "Have a great time and don't drink too much! You've got your work tomorrow!"

"I know – spoilsport!" she said jokingly. "Don't wait up though. Charlene said something about getting the last train home."

Peter raised his eyebrows. "Don't worry, I won't," he said, smiling to himself. *Perfect!*

~

The Abbotsford Hotel was relatively quiet compared to the weekends. Claire and Charlene were guided to their table in the far corner of the long, narrow restaurant and were pleased that no one was sitting near them.

"This is lovely, Claire," said Charlene, taking off her coat and sitting down.

Claire could see that Charlene had not changed a bit; she was dressed in bright-coloured clothing from head to toe, with bright red hair to match. Claire was the complete opposite; she wore a plain navy blue, knee-length dress with flat black shoes. Her natural-coloured brown hair was neatly tied up in a short ponytail, as she didn't have time to wash and dry it before rushing out to meet Charlene at the station.

Once seated and settled in, the pair were greeted by Jamie, the affable owner of the hotel, who ran the establishment with a rod of steel along with his sister, Senga. "Hello Claire, good to see you again. And who is this stranger?"

"Jamie, this is Charlene Tannock, a friend of mine."

"It's a pleasure," he said, offering to shake hands with Charlene.

Charlene noticed the absence of a wedding ring and responded. "The pleasure is all mine," she said, winking at Jamie, whose face immediately turned bright red.

Claire couldn't believe Charlene was so brazen and burst out laughing.

"I'll, eh, send someone over to take your order in a few minutes," he said and left the two ladies giggling at the table.

"Charlene – what are you like? You've scared the poor man off. He'll not be back now."

"That's a pity! I rather liked him. Oh well, let's order a bottle of wine and see what happens. White or red?"

Claire hummed and hawed. "I don't care, you choose." She leant over the table, picked up the wine menu and passed it to Charlene, who smiled and accepted it gracefully.

After some consideration, Charlene decided to go for the most expensive bottle of red on the menu and could see that Claire was a little taken aback by her choice. "It'll be my treat!"

"No, I couldn't possibly accept. Honestly, it's fine, we'll share it."

"No, we will not. I know how little you police officers get paid. It's an utter disgrace! Please let me pay for the wine. We can share the cost of the meal."

Claire could tell that Charlene was not going to back down. "Okay, you win. Let's order the wine and food. I'm starving."

~

Peter had walked Sally and was now preparing to visit Wallace. He was dressed in black and was busy packing a small bag with black gloves, a black balaclava and a few other items that he thought might be useful.

He locked Sally in the kitchen and made his way out the backdoor to the back lane where he had parked his car. He got in and drove off, confident that none of his neighbours had seen him. *So far, so good!*

Chapter 33

Charlene knew that Claire wanted to speak about Peter but could sense she was not quite ready to share. A large glass of wine would help! She topped up both wine glasses and chose a subject she knew Claire would be more than happy to discuss. "So, Claire, tell me all about your current case. I'm fascinated to know what's been going on."

Claire looked around to check that no one in the restaurant could overhear the conversation. "I admit, I've not had a case quite like it. We've had so many different suspects to track down and interview, it's been a bit overwhelming. It's just as well we're getting help from MIT as we just wouldn't have the resources to conduct an investigation of this scale on our own."

"So, you're working with Carter again?"

This prompted Claire to ask the question that she had been desperate to ask for some time. "Yes, and sorry for asking, but has there ever been anything more than a professional relationship between you and Carter?"

"Do you mean – have we been seeing each other?" asked Charlene.

Claire nodded.

"Was it that obvious?"

"Well… I am a copper. It's my job to spot that sort of stuff."

Charlene smiled at Claire. "Well, you're right. We did go out for a while. I really like Carter, but he just couldn't open up fully to me and commit to the relationship. I blame it on that bloody war."

"War?" asked Claire.

"Yes. Before he joined the police, he was in the army and served in Iraq. That's how he got that scar on his face."

"Oh! I thought it must have happened to him while serving as a police officer. So, what happened?"

"Well, Carter doesn't really talk about it unless you get him drunk and believe me, that requires a lot of alcohol. But he did share some things with me. You see, Carter was an M.P., a military policeman, and it was his job to keep the troops in order whenever they let off steam. You can imagine the pressure those soldiers must have been under. Anyway, to cut things short, he was breaking up a bar fight between two British soldiers when one of them pulled out a knife and slashed him."

"Oh my God!" said Claire. "It must have been awful. Bad enough dealing with the enemy, but when your own men turn on you..."

"I'm quite sure that's why Carter is the way he is. You know, all rough and tough, barks orders at everyone and has the shortest fuse known to man."

Claire laughed, acknowledging the perfectly accurate characterisation of DCI Carter. "That explains a lot."

"Yes, so enough about my man—well, my ex. What about your man, Peter? What's he been up to?"

Chapter 34

Peter parked his car a few streets away from Wallace's house. He opened his bag, put on the gloves, stuffed the balaclava into his jacket pocket and put the bag over his shoulder. Looking around to see if anyone had seen him, he quickly locked the car and walked briskly towards Wallace's house.

After a few minutes, he reached the driveway and looked up at the house. He could see that the lights were on, and that there was movement upstairs in what he assumed was the master bedroom. *Good!* He looked around, checked that no one was looking and then skipped up the path, but instead of going to the front door, he headed for the back of the house and found the back door. He pulled down his balaclava to hide his face and tried the door handle. The door was locked. It was an old-fashioned wooden door with a glass panel on the top to let some light into the room. Peter looked down through the glass and saw with a smile that the keys were still in the door. He opened his bag and took out a small hammer—he knew that Wallace would hear the breaking of the glass and come rushing into the kitchen, but that was fine. As long as Peter got inside first, that was all that mattered.

Wallace was upstairs in his bedroom, getting changed. He always wore a suit to work but never at home. As he pulled a fresh t-shirt over his head, he heard the noise of breaking glass coming from downstairs. *What the hell was that?* He ran downstairs in his stocking soles, almost slipping on the last two carpeted steps. He steadied himself and entered the kitchen where, to his shock, she saw the man dressed in black from head to toe. His heart almost stopped. "Jesus Christ! What the…"

"Sit down, Wallace," instructed Peter, pointing to one of the chairs on the other side of the kitchen table.

"What? No! Get out of my house, or I'll call the police!" Wallace shouted.

"Oh, I don't think Mr Baxter would like that, do you?"

"Baxter! Who on earth is... oh, that Mr Baxter, what does he want? I don't work for Petrie anymore. He's dead."

Peter smiled to himself. This was going exactly as he had planned. "Take a seat, Mr Wallace. I'm not going to hurt you, providing you tell me everything that I want to know." It was a lie, but Wallace didn't need to know that.

Wallace looked at the man who stood in the way of the backdoor and then glanced at the kitchen door. He thought about running to the front door to escape, but looking at the man's build and judging by his voice, it was clear that he was both younger and fitter than Wallace, so his chances of out-running him were slim. In the absence of any meaningful options, Wallace decided to do as he was told and sat down.

Peter remained on his feet. "Good decision. Now, Mr Baxter wants to know who put out the hit on Detective Inspector Claire Redding."

"What? But surely he must know already. After all, McCafferty works for him now and he ordered the hit."

"McCafferty? Where can I find him?"

Wallace suddenly realised that something was wrong. "You don't work for Baxter, do you? Who are you?" Wallace looked around the kitchen in a panic, his eye catching the set of kitchen knives on the worktop near the gas hob. He jumped off his seat and threw himself at the worktop, managing to grasp a large carving knife.

Peter was too slow to stop Wallace from reaching the knife, but was able to grab him from behind. Wallace tried his best to twist his body to turn the blade towards Peter, but he was stronger than Wallace and grabbed the arm holding the weapon. He then twisted Wallace's arm around behind his back, almost to breaking point. Wallace screamed in pain and dropped the knife, which clattered against the tiled floor and bounced into the corner behind Peter.

In desperation, his adrenaline now taking over, Wallace swung a punch at Peter, which glanced off his skull, barely making contact. Peter responded in kind but caught Wallace square on the jaw, snapping his head to the left. Wallace was stunned, and Peter hit him again, this time with even more force than the first. Wallace blacked out, falling onto the hard and unforgiving floor. When he came round, Wallace was sitting on a kitchen chair. His hands had been tied behind his back with rope and his ankles were bound together with heavy tape that Peter had taken from his bag.

Wallace opened his eyes and stared with fright at Peter who was now holding the large carving knife in his hand. "Okay, Wallace. I want answers. Who is this McCafferty and where can I find him?"

Wallace knew it was pointless pretending to be brave—he was petrified. "Okay, you win. McCafferty used to manage Petrie's pub in the East End, the Dog and Bone. I'm not sure if he's still there, but he's the one you're after. He ordered the hit on the young policewoman. I… I tried to stop it, but he said he couldn't; the money had been sent and that was that. Honestly, I didn't want her to be hurt, not after Petrie was killed."

"But you passed on the message, didn't you? You took Petrie's message from him in prison and passed it to McCafferty. Didn't you?" shouted Peter, his anger turning to rage.

Wallace nodded slowly and dropped his head in shame, tears now streaming from his eyes. "I'm sorry, I really am, but she's alright, isn't she? She survived. I read it in the paper."

Peter stood up and bashed the table with his right fist which made Wallace flinch with fright. "And did you read about the baby that she lost? Did you read that in the newspapers?" screamed Peter. The painful memory of the hospital scene was now replaying rapidly in his mind, eating away at his soul—reigniting the uncontrollable rage that he had felt that day.

Wallace was filled with dread at the sudden realisation of who was standing before him wielding a carving knife. "You… You are her husband. The father of the child! Oh no, oh God."

"I don't believe in God, Mr Wallace, but I hope for your sake that he's listening." Peter stuck the knife through the man's chest, slicing open his heart, plunging deep enough to cut into his backbone, severing the spinal nerve. Peter watched as the life drained from Wallace's face and then carefully pulled out the blood covered blade. Wallace's head fell forward. His death had been quicker than Peter had thought and he now regretted going straight for his heart. It took a moment for Peter to appreciate the enormity of the act that he had just committed. He was temporarily overcome by a mix of fear and adrenaline but he steadied himself. Now was not the time to panic. He needed to keep a cool head and see out the rest of his plan.

Peter wiped the knife on Wallace's t-shirt, took it to the sink and rinsed it clean. He then put it back with the others in the knife block. He retrieved a Stanley knife from his bag and then carefully cut off the rope and tape from Wallace's hands and feet, rolling it all up into a ball and putting it in his bag.

He stood up, looked around and went over to the gas hob. He turned on one of the gas burners, and as he had thought, the burner knob had to be turned and held in to release gas. This position also prompted the burner to spark and ignite. He found the electrical switch which powered the hob's ignition system and turned it off. He then returned to his bag and removed the heavy roll of Duct Tape. He carefully cut a long piece of tape and stuck down all four switches in the on position, thus allowing the gas to escape freely. He then took a timer switch from his bag, plugged it into the wall next to the toaster and set it to turn on in exactly one hour. Peter stuffed some paper towels into the toaster, cut another piece of Duct Tape and stuck down the toaster's lever so it was in the on-position, but without any power. He carefully plugged the toaster into the timer and was pleased to see that nothing happened. That would come later: the power would come on and the paper would ignite, hopefully causing an explosion strong enough to blow the house apart and destroy any evidence that he had ever been there. The perfect crime!

Chapter 35

Claire poured herself another glass of wine to give herself time to think about how she would tell Charlene about Peter and then decided to blurt it all out. "I think Peter paid for a gangster called Petrie to be killed."

Charlene was visibly stunned. "What? Peter killed who?"

"Sorry, I should have explained. It all happened before I knew you—Petrie was a Glasgow drug lord. I was responsible for his imprisonment, and so he threatened to kill me and my family if I didn't withdraw my statement and refuse to testify. Peter was terrified and didn't tell me about it at first. It was the same day that I found out I was pregnant, and he didn't...."

"Oh God!" was all Charlene could think to say in response.

Claire continued, now keen to get it all off her chest. "He didn't want to ruin the joy of the news of the baby you see. I scolded him for being so silly and told him I wasn't afraid of Petrie, but I should have been—it was Petrie who ordered my assassination."

Charlene was astounded. "Oh, I remember now, but according to the news reports, Petrie died in prison."

Claire nodded and stared at Charlene, waiting for her to make the connection.

"Oh! So, you think that Peter somehow managed to get Petrie killed in jail," Charlene said incredulously.

"Yes."

Charlene was lost for words, but not for long as her brain started to fire up and threw out several glaring questions which needed to be answered. "And what makes you think Peter had anything to do with it? Do you have any evidence?"

"Well, not evidence as such, but hear me out before you say anything. The Organised

Crime Team in Glasgow traced a payment to one of Petrie's enemies, a gangster called Baxter, whom they believe organised the hit on Petrie. The payment came from a company called 'P&SMAC Holdings Ltd.', and because I had been involved with the case, they asked me if I recognised the name."

Charlene looked even more confused, so Claire went on to explain. "At first, I didn't have a clue and told them so, but then it came to me, while jogging. P&SMAC could be short for Peter and Sally Macdonald."

"Sally?" asked Charlene, still not getting it.

"Peter has a dog called Sally," explained Claire.

"Right, and your whole theory is based on that connection. There's no other evidence?"

"Well, Peter is a stockbroker. He knows all about moving money around and could easily set up a false company and bank account to facilitate the transaction. And, he has made a lot of money selling shares."

"Yes, but you said it yourself, Claire. There's no hard evidence. I hope you haven't mentioned any of this Peter."

"No, of course not, but I'm convinced he's involved. I just can't prove it."

"Okay, let's try and rationalise this," offered Charlene. "Now, I know you are a police officer, and the law is the law, but what if you are wrong? What if this is just a coincidence? Are you prepared to ruin your marriage on this suspicion of guilt? Because that's what all this comes down to in the end."

Deep down Claire knew that Charlene was right. She just found it difficult to ignore her gut feeling.

"Do you still love him?" asked Charlene.

Claire sighed. "Yes, I do, and it's killing me."

"So, the best thing you can do is put all these doubts and suspicions behind you. Bury yourself in your work if that is what it takes but hold on to your marriage with both hands and let time take care of the rest. That's my advice."

Claire smiled. "Yes, doctor."

~

Peter sat in his car shaking; the adrenaline rush that he had felt in the kitchen was now subsiding, and his heart rate was slowly returning to normal. He hadn't been sure if he would be strong enough to go through with it – to kill another human being – but he was glad he did. *Wallace was just as guilty as Petrie and got what he deserved.*

He checked his watch, started the car and headed home, confident that he would get there in plenty of time to dispose of his clothes, shower, and get into bed before Claire got home. In the morning, he would scan the news channels for reports on a gas explosion in Glasgow and then begin to plan how he would deal with McCafferty. He knew that was going to be a much tougher proposition.

~

Claire walked Charlene to the train station, waved her off onto the last train to Glasgow and then headed home along Glasgow Road. Charlene had given her a lot to think about, and perhaps she had been right, perhaps Claire should let sleeping dogs lie and allow time to heal the bond between her and Peter.

By the time Claire had reached the front door, she had made up her mind. She would take Charlene's advice and try to move on with her life. She looked up at the bedroom window where she knew Peter would be sleeping soundly at this time of night and noticed that, as always, he had left her bedside lamp on so she wouldn't make a noise getting herself into bed in the dark.

Claire entered the house, her home, gently closed the door behind her and locked it. She removed her shoes and crept upstairs, keen not to disturb Peter and Sally. She entered the bedroom and could see that Peter was sleeping in his usual position: on his side, facing the window. She quickly undressed, put on her pyjamas and slipped into bed without disturbing him. *Mission accomplished!*

Peter had heard her come in but thought it wiser to pretend to be asleep. It would support the theory and potential alibi, if one was needed, that he was home all night and had gone to bed early. As he lay there, he reviewed all his actions that night—going over and over in his head what had happened and, more importantly, if he had made any mistakes. The only small fly in the ointment was that his neighbours—the Browns, had spotted him coming home and although he hadn't planned on it, he had already thought up an excuse for being out that evening, if needed. Eventually he fell into a deep sleep, confident that he was in the clear.

Chapter 36

Peter was first to get up the next morning. He had deliberately set his alarm early to give the impression that he had a long sleep, but more importantly, he was eager to hear the news about the explosion.

He made his way into the kitchen and put on the radio. He had it set to BBC Radio Scotland and knew that there would be regular news updates throughout the morning. The two morning presenters were talking about a new species of mammal discovered in the hills of Indonesia, so Peter decided to put on the kettle to make himself a coffee and wait for the news.

Sally, who was still a bit tired, meandered over to Peter to greet him in her usual way—nosing his hand. She was getting a bit older now, and the once feisty little Cocker Spaniel was far more laid back than the young, excitable dog that he had brought into his home all those years ago. Greeting over, she returned to her bed and flopped down onto the soft pillow.

Peter sat at the kitchen table, coffee in hand, and waited patiently for the news. He didn't have to wait long, and unsurprisingly, the explosion in Glasgow was the top news story of the morning. According to the reporter at the scene, the fire service had been there throughout the night and had to evacuate a few nearby houses, such was the severity of the blast and the fire. The fire service had confirmed that the explosion appeared to be caused by a gas leak at the back of the property, but as the structure of the two-storey house had completely collapsed in on itself, it would be several days before fire investigators would be able to carry out a thorough inspection of the property. The reporter went on to explain that the police had confirmed that the house was occupied by a single male, a local solicitor, whose body had yet to be found.

Peter sipped at his coffee and smiled to himself, satisfied that his plan had worked and confident that there was no way that the crime could now be linked to him. He jumped a little, when the kitchen door suddenly opened.

"Hello, you're up early," said Claire, as she entered the kitchen.

"Yes, I've got a busy day ahead and wanted to make an early start. What time did you get in last night?"

Claire walked over the kettle and switched it on. "About twelve. Charlene just made the last train."

"Did you have a good night?" asked Peter.

"Yes, it was good to get out again and chill."

"What did you talk about?"

"Oh, you know, the usual stuff that we ladies talk about."

"Oh, yeah? And what would that be?"

"Men."

"Men? What, you were talking about me?"

"Of course."

"And what did you say?" Peter was genuinely interested to know.

Claire was enjoying teasing him, and it appeared that he was happy to play along. It had been a while since Claire had been so relaxed in his company. "Oh, you know, the usual stuff!" She sat down at the table, smiled and sipped at her coffee.

"The usual stuff?"

"Yes, how much you snore and all the other little things that endear you men to us women."

Peter grinned. "I see. And what about Charlene? Does she have a man?"

"Not at the moment, but she did have a fling with Carter at one point."

"Really!"

"Yes, and she shared some interesting stories about him. Apparently, Carter served in Iraq. He was a military policeman."

"Blimey! I don't envy him that experience. I heard it was pretty bad out there."

Claire nodded. "Yip. That's where he got his scar." She ran a finger up the side of her face to emphasise the point. "Apparently it was one of his own soldiers that did it. Charlene reckons the whole experience has changed him. Made him harder."

"I bet it did," said Peter, thinking back to events in his own past that had changed him. He had almost killed another boy when he was in residential care. The boy had stolen from Peter and they had gotten into a fight. If it hadn't been for one of the staff's timely intervention, Peter would have strangled the boy to death. It hadn't been long after Peter's mother had died so the manager of the home decided to be lenient and let Peter off. Normally, he would have been referred to the Children's Panel which would have gone on his record but thankfully it hadn't. However, Peter knew the truth. He knew he had the mentality needed to take another's life, and now he had.

Claire could see that Peter's mind had wandered off for a moment. "Where did you go just then?"

"Sorry, I was just thinking back to my time in residential care."

"And did it change you?" asked Claire.

"Yes, I suppose it did," Peter said reflectively.

"You never talk about it."

"I know, but it wasn't a good time in my life so I prefer to leave it where it belongs—in the past. It's how I deal with things. Anyway, enough of this idle chit chat. I'm going up to have a shower and get ready for work."

"Are you not going to have any breakfast?"

"Nah, I'm not hungry."

"Okay, but don't be too long in there. I have a briefing at eight."

Peter nodded and headed upstairs.

Claire knew there was no point pushing the issue; she had tried before and failed. Whatever had happened to him in that care home must have been serious, but he just wouldn't talk about it. In some ways, Peter was a bit like Carter—full of secrets.

Chapter 37

The morning briefing had been short and sharp. Carter had barked orders to most of the team and was preparing to interview McLeish, who was scheduled to arrive at 8.30 a.m. Claire had been asked to prepare questions for the interviews with Donaldson's cleaner and gardener—they had been asked to come in after nine o'clock for questioning. She had finally managed to contact them before going home last night.

Carter had also decided to be proactive and had instructed Paul and Jim to pay James Johnston a visit at his farm. Carter wanted to know if Johnston owned any tractors with a similar-sized wheelbase to the tracks found at the crime scene. They were still waiting on the forensic report specifying the exact make and model of the tractor, but Carter didn't want to wait. Consequently, Paul was given the measurements and told to bring Johnston in for further questioning if they found a match.

~

McLeish arrived at the station at precisely 8.30 a.m. and was immediately taken up to interview room one, where Claire and Carter were waiting. McLeish appeared to be in his late fifties and was wearing a black woollen coat over a light-grey suit. He undid his coat to reveal a bright blue tie and a crisp white shirt, all of which looked to be expensive, but not as expensive as the Rolex watch he was wearing on his left wrist.

After some brief introductions, Carter began the interview. "Mr McLeish, you will be aware that Michael Donaldson, MSP was found dead, hanging from a tree last Monday morning."

McLeish nodded. "Yes, terrible news, and I understand from this morning's newspaper reports that it wasn't suicide."

"Yes, that's correct. We are treating it as a suspicious death and are investigating accordingly."

"I assume I'm not a suspect?" asked McLeish.

"No, we are simply trying to gather as much information about Mr Donaldson as possible, and therefore we are speaking to everyone who knew him."

"Yes, but I'm not sure how I can be of any help, Inspector."

"It's Chief Inspector, "Carter corrected.

"Sorry, Chief Inspector," responded McLeish.

"Your name was mentioned on a report that we found in Mr Donaldson's briefcase," said Carter. "Can you explain why he would write your name on the report?"

"I've no idea, Inspect… Sorry, Chief Inspector."

"That's strange. We also found an e-mail from Mr Donaldson to you on the night he died. How do you explain that?"

"Again, I have no idea why Mike would want to contact me. What was the report about?"

Claire decided to intervene. "The report was about a proposal to build a new relief road connecting Dumbarton to Glasgow. Why would Mr Donaldson want to speak to you about the proposal?"

"I've no idea. Perhaps he wanted my advice. We're old friends—we went to university together."

Carter could see that this line of questioning was going nowhere. "What line of business are you in, Mr McLeish?"

"Construction."

"It's a bit of a coincidence that the government is planning to build a new road, and the government minister wants to speak to the owner of a construction company. Don't you think so?" asked Carter. He knew he was fishing.

"As I said before, I have no idea why Mike would want to speak to me."

"Are you friends with Mrs Donaldson?" asked Claire.

"What? No, what are you implying, Inspector?"

"I'm not implying anything, Mr McLeish. Please answer the question."

"No, I've never met her," he said sharply.

"One final question, Mr McLeish. Where were you between the hours of midnight and 4 a.m. last Monday morning?" asked Carter.

"I thought I wasn't a suspect," responded McLeish.

"You're not, but I would still like you to answer the question."

"I was down south on business. Stayed overnight at a hotel in Manchester."

"And someone will be able to confirm this?" asked Carter.

"I'm sure there'll be plenty of people at the hotel who can confirm it. Hold on." McLeish removed his phone from his pocket and scrolled down his emails. "Ah, here it is! Confirmation of the hotel booking. The details are all there." He passed his phone to Carter who in turn passed it to Claire. She checked the information and took a few notes in her pad, then returned the phone to McLeish.

"Right, thank you for coming in Mr McLeish. DI Redding will see you out."

McLeish fastened his coat and followed DI Redding out of the room. Carter couldn't help but notice the smug look on his face. *The smug bastard was hiding something*!

Claire returned to the interview room and headed over to Carter. "Well, sir? What do you think?"

"If his alibi stands up, then he's in the clear for the murder. We don't even have a motive."

"Yes, but he's hiding something, I could sense it. I'm just not sure what exactly."

"It wouldn't surprise me if he and Donaldson were in cahoots over this road project—there's big money involved. Maybe Donaldson was getting a bung for leaking inside information?"

"That's going to be pretty hard to prove," said Claire. "Do you want me to give the fraud team the heads up?"

"I don't see the harm, but in the meantime get Doyle to check out the hotel. Now, let's grab a quick cup of tea before the cleaner gets here. I'm gasping."

Chapter 38

"Hello, Mrs Muldoon, I'm Detective Chief Inspector Carter and this is Detective Inspector Redding. Thank you for taking the trouble to come and speak to us."

Mrs Muldoon looked at both detectives and smiled awkwardly. It was clear that she was extremely nervous; she sat bolt upright in the chair with both hands gripping the strap of her handbag. Judging by her greying hair and wrinkled skin, Claire estimated that the woman was in her sixties. However, despite her obvious years, the woman looked very fit, most probably a consequence of her employment as a cleaner.

Carter could sense the woman's nervousness and tried to put her at ease. "Mrs Muldoon, you will be aware that the reason why you are here is because we are investigating the death of Mr Donaldson but please be assured that you're not a suspect and are not under arrest."

She nodded slowly confirming that she understood so Carter decided just to get on with it and put the poor woman out of her misery. "How long have you been working for the Donaldsons?" he asked.

The woman looked down at her handbag and appeared to be counting in her head. Much to the amusement of both detectives, she stopped and started again and then nodded to her herself. "Forty-three years," she whispered.

"Oh! So you would have worked for Mr Donaldson's parents?" asked Claire.

"Yes, that's right. They were lovely people."

"And your current employers. Are they lovely people?" asked Carter.

The question clearly bothered the elderly cleaner. "I'm not sure I should say. It's not right to speak ill of the dead."

"So, you didn't like Mr Donaldson then?"

"I didn't say that. I didn't have many dealings with Mr Donaldson. It was Mrs Donaldson who gave me my instructions and paid me."

"I see. Would you say you have a good working relationship with Mrs Donaldson?"

"Yes, she's pleasant enough."

"Okay, thanks." Carter nodded to Claire to indicate that she could take over.

"Mrs Muldoon, I understand that when you spoke to my colleague, Sergeant O'Neill, you said that you usually clean the house every Friday but last Friday you had a family funeral. Is that correct?"

Tears started to form in the corners of the woman's eyes. "Yes, my oldest brother Tommy died the week before."

"I'm sorry to hear that," said Claire with genuine sincerity. "When did you notify Mrs Donaldson that you would not be able to clean on Friday?"

"As soon as the funeral had been arranged. It was on Monday of that week."

"When you spoke to Mrs Donaldson, did she suggest that you clean on the following Monday or was that your suggestion?"

"Oh dear. Now let me think. Ah yes, I remember now. I offered to come in on Thursday but she said not to bother myself before the funeral and come in on Monday instead. That was nice of her."

"Yes, it was," agreed Claire. I also understand that you cleaned the ground floor first. Is that correct?"

"Yes."

"Do you normally clean the ground floor first?"

"No, I usually start at the top and work my way down."

"So, why do it differently this time?"

"I started at six that morning as I have another house to clean on a Monday afternoon and I didn't want to disturb Mrs Donaldson."

"Was that your suggestion or hers?"

Mrs Muldoon paused momentarily to think about it. "Sorry, I can't remember whose idea it was but it made sense."

"Right. So, on Monday morning at six a.m., you let yourself in? I assume you have a key."

"Yes, I have a key to the backdoor."

"And was the backdoor locked that morning?"

"Sorry, I can't remember."

"Is it usually locked?"

"No, but then I don't usually arrive before ten and everyone in the house would be up and about."

Claire kicked herself for asking such a daft question. "Of course. Makes sense. When you cleaned the study did you notice anything suspicious?"

Mrs Muldoon hesitated. "No, I don't think so."

"The room was extremely clean," Claire remarked. "Is that the normal level of cleaning that you provide?"

"Of course, I take great pride in my work."

"Right. And did you also clean the decanter and glasses?" asked Claire.

"I would if it were obvious if they had been used. You know, dirty glasses left in the tray. I would take them to the kitchen and clean them and return them to tray."

"And the decanter?"

"I would give it a wipe down. Ever since the COVID pandemic, I'm careful to ensure good hygiene. I wear gloves when I clean." This was not the answer Claire had been hoping for but nevertheless it did explain the pristine condition of the room.

Claire turned to Carter to indicate that it was his turn to ask the final few questions.

"Mrs Muldoon, does Mrs Donaldson have any visitors to the house?"

"Sometimes."

"Do you know who they are?"

"It's not really any of my business, is it?"

"No, but this is a murder investigation and it is our business to know, so I'd appreciate it if you would answer the question."

"Well, she does have some friends visit her on occasion. I think they play tennis or something. And then there's the gardener, of course. Oh, I did notice another gentleman around the house but he might have been there to see Mr Donaldson—he was wearing a suit."

Carter sat up, suddenly taking a keen interest in her response. "This man wearing a suit, can you describe him?"

~

Peter was sitting in the Dog and Bone public house in the east end of Glasgow, slowly nursing a soft drink which he had ordered over an hour ago. He pretended to read a newspaper and had deliberately sat near the bar so he could overhear the bar staff chat. So far, there had been no mention of McCafferty and he was beginning to wonder if this was the best way to approach things. He could, of course, be bold and ask for him by name but he didn't want to draw any attention to himself. No, he would need to be patient and sit tight. He had taken the full day off work, just in case, and decided that he would probably need to order more drinks and perhaps lunch to maintain his deception and avoid suspicion. He leaned over and took a copy of the menu out of the wooden holder to see if there was anything that took his fancy. Having quickly scanned it, he opted for steak pie and chips and then returned the menu. He got up and ordered another drink—that would tide him over to lunchtime.

Chapter 39

Mrs Muldoon's description of the man in the suit had matched that of Mr Malcolm Munro and had prompted Carter to instruct Brian to get Munro back in for further questioning. In the meantime, Carter and Claire were sitting in interview room two, awaiting the arrival of Callum Maclean, Donaldson's gardener.

Mr Maclean was not what the two detectives were expecting. For a start, he was not in his sixties. For some reason, both detectives were expecting a man of similar age to Mrs Muldoon, but the handsome, well-tanned, well-groomed man who stood before them was quite the opposite.

As agreed, Claire did the introductions and commenced the questioning. "Mr Maclean, how long have you worked for the Donaldsons?"

"Well, that depends on what you mean by working for them. You see, I helped my dad out when I was a teenager and when he passed, I took over his gardening business."

"Oh, I'm sorry to hear that. So, how long has it been since your father died?"

"Just over twenty years ago."

"Right, so you would have worked for Michael Donaldson's parents before Michael took over the property."

"Yes, that's correct."

"And how well did you know Michael Donaldson?"

"Not that well. I knew him as a boy, but we never played together as he was a bit older than me. I was friends with his younger brother, David—we were about the same age and went to school together."

"And Mrs Donaldson? How well do you know her?"

"Not that well, but she does take a keen interest in the garden, so we often chat about the choice of shrubs, flowers and plants. I advise her on the type of plant that would suit the soil, their position in the garden and so on."

"You certainly know your stuff. It's a beautiful garden!" Claire commented.

"Thank you. It's nice that someone other than Mrs Donaldson appreciates it."

"It must take you a long time to get it looking so good, especially in summer."

"It can do, but I have a lot of equipment which helps," he replied.

Claire nodded. "Sounds like you must spend quite a lot of time around the grounds and at the house. Have you noticed any strangers around recently?"

"No, I don't think so."

"What about visitors? Does Mrs Donaldson get any visitors?"

Maclean suddenly realised what Claire was getting at. "You mean *male* visitors, Inspector. Well, I did notice one man enter the house on a few occasions in recent weeks. He was in his forties, quite good-looking, well-tanned and was wearing a suit." Maclean went on to give a similar description to the one provided earlier by Mrs Muldoon. It was obvious to Claire and Carter that they had both described Malcolm Munro.

Chapter 40

Peter had waited another hour without success and decided it was time to order some lunch. He grabbed the menu and approached the bar. He caught the eye of one of the two bar staff who were on duty that day, and he immediately came over to serve him.

"What can I get you?" asked the bartender.

"Could I order some food, please?"

"Sure, what would you like?"

"The steak pie, please."

"With chips or mashed potatoes?"

"Chips, please."

The bartender tapped the order into the pad on the till. "That'll be £9.99, do you want any more drinks?"

"Yes, a soda water and lime, please."

"No problem. That'll be £12.99 in total. Card or cash?"

"Cash."

Peter removed £15 from his wallet and handed it to the bartender, who opened the till and took out the change. "Here you are." The bartender looked behind Peter. "Oh, hi there, Danny."

Peter turned and saw the man the bartender was addressing. It suddenly struck him that this could be the same Daniel McCafferty that he had been looking for. He turned back to the bartender, took his change and went and sat down at his table, keeping his focus on the bar.

McCafferty approached the bar. "I'll be upstairs if anyone is looking for me."

"No problem, boss," replied the bartender.

Boss? He must be McCafferty, thought Peter.

McCafferty went through the connecting door to the toilets, and Peter decided to follow him. He still wasn't entirely sure that this was the man that he was after but he was determined to find out. He went through the connecting door, headed for the gents' toilets and spotted McCafferty going up the stairs on his right. He waited until the man was out of sight and then slowly climbed the stairs, careful not to make any noise. When he reached the upper landing, he could see a door with a small sign: 'Private—Staff Only.' Peter made his way carefully towards the door and could hear a man's voice. He put his ear to the door and listened to the one-sided conversation. The man was on the telephone.

"Hoy! What are you up to?"

Peter was startled and turned quickly to see the young bartender who had just served him. "Sorry, I was looking for the toilets," said Peter apologetically and backed away from the door.

The bartender sneered at Peter. "Well, you'll not find them in there—that's Mr McCafferty's Office. Can't you read? It says *private*. The toilets are downstairs."

"Right, sorry, I'll just go then… and find them."

"Yeah, you do that!"

It was clear the bartender didn't really buy his story, but Peter didn't care about that—he just wanted to avoid being seen by the man who he now knew was McCafferty. Peter practically leapt down the stairs as fast as he could without tripping and went straight back into the bar area where his meal was waiting for him.

Great! Microwaved pub grub. He picked up the cutlery which had been wrapped in a napkin and cut into the crusty steak pie.

Chapter 41

Claire and Carter were sitting in the staff cafeteria, both eating macaroni cheese. It was one of the few meals that passed the *barely edible* test unless they opted for the less healthy option of a roll and sausage or a roll and bacon, or both—the latter was known in the station as a double heart attack on a bun. There was the healthier option of a salad—if you could call a few limp lettuce leaves, some chopped tomatoes and red onion a salad—but neither detective fancied the look of it. Even Claire, who would normally opt for the healthy option, couldn't quite force herself to take the sad-looking salad.

Claire finished her last mouthful of macaroni and then checked her watch. "What time is Munro due to get here?"

"Brian said he should make it in for about one thirty. We have time for a coffee. Do you want one?"

"Yes, please. Black, no sugar."

Carter went to the servery and ordered two coffees. Claire checked the messages on her phone and noticed a text from Peter saying that he had gone into the office. She quickly texted him back. 'No problem' and then, after some thought, added an 'x'. A small sign that she was at least going to try and make their relationship work.

Carter returned with the coffees and sat down. "So, Malcolm Munro, how do you want to play it?"

Claire had been thinking about this while eating her macaroni and was still unsure of how to handle him. "Well, first, he'll need to explain why he made those visits to the house. And, if we're not satisfied with his response, we can try to push him on the issue of his relationship with Mrs Donaldson."

Carter nodded. "And if he doesn't give us anything…"

"If he doesn't open up, then I'm not sure we have anything to use against him. We don't even have a motive unless we can connect him to Mrs Donaldson. I know he appears to be a suspect, but…"

"But what, Claire? Come on… spill it?"

"Well, I just don't see him and Mrs Donaldson being together. Now the gardener, Callum Maclean! He's a completely different kettle of fish. I could see the attraction there— call it feminine intuition if you must, but that's how I see it."

"So, you fancy him, do you?" said Carter grinning.

"No, don't be daft." Claire's face turned a little red, and then something flashed across her mind – something so glaringly obvious that she was astonished it had not occurred to her as soon as she had seen the handsome gardener.

Carter could see the spark in her eyes. "What?"

"What if Mrs Donaldson is having an affair with Maclean?"

"Now there's a proper motive for murder," said Carter. Okay, let's look at that as a possibility. If he studied gardening at college, he would have a good knowledge of botany and poisonous plants, so let's get that checked."

Claire smiled, excited that she may have just stumbled upon the killer by accident—the actual killer, with both motive and the means. "And there's something else we should check before we bring him back in—does he own a small tractor?"

"You're right. If we can match the tractor tyres… No, hold on, it would be even better if we could also match a soil sample taken from the tyres with a soil sample from the field, but we'll need a warrant to get that. Then he'll have a much more challenging time explaining that one to the jury. Right, first things first. Let's get them both in here for questioning. We can try to play them off each other and see if either of them breaks. Let's see if he has the tractor that we're looking for, and if so, then he's our prime suspect."

"But what about Munro? He's on his way in," said Claire.

"We'll get Rambo and Doyle to question him. Wouldn't want him to feel the journey was a waste of his time. And besides, he still needs to explain why he was at the house."

Claire looked concerned. "Rambo? Is he the right person? I know he's a sergeant, but he's not exactly a people person, is he?"

Carter knew exactly what Claire was getting at. "Fine, we'll let your boys deal with him, Paul and Jim, isn't it?"

"Yes, they're both experienced interviewers. I'll give them some pointers as I still believe there's a connection between Munro and McLeish. I wonder if Rambo has found anything else in Donaldson's emails which might give them something to use?"

"Did you ever make that call to the fraud squad?" asked Carter.

"Yes, but they didn't think we had enough evidence to warrant an investigation."

"Yeah, probably right. Let's hope your boys manage to get something out of him that we can give to the fraud team. If Donaldson was involved in something illegal before he died, I would want the world to know about it. The way things are going, he'll be treated like a hero, a political saint who could do no wrong. Well, we know differently, don't we? The press would love that story."

"Carter, you're not serious... are you?" asked Claire worriedly.

Carter grinned at Claire mischievously, "What do you think?"

Chapter 42

Claire and Carter entered the incident room and immediately went about issuing new instructions to the team. After speaking to Jim and Paul about Munro, Claire headed over to Brian to share their latest thinking on the case. Brian was sat at his desk studying the screen of his laptop. He was reading the forensic update on the tractor tyre tracks found at the scene.

"The forensic report came in while you were at lunch. They think they've got a match on the tractor. It looks like the one we're interested in is a John Deere X350R. It's used to…"

"Cut grass," said Claire smugly.

"Yes, how did you know?"

"Because I had a bit of an epiphany at lunchtime. Carter and I now think it is more likely that Mrs Donaldson was having an affair with the gardener, Callum Maclean. It would explain the poisonous plants and..."

"The tractor, of course."

"Yes, but it's all very circumstantial so we're bringing them both in for further questioning. If Maclean confirms that he owns the same tractor, we can get a search warrant to search his property and take samples from the mud on his tractor wheels. With any luck, it will match and we'll have him."

"Yeah, but it still wouldn't be enough to convict Mrs Donaldson. If he loves her enough to kill for her then he's not going to implicate her, even if he does go down for the murder charge."

"True, which is why Carter wants them both brought in and interviewed simultaneously. Take their statements and see if we catch them both out in a lie."

"I guess that's why I'm only a sergeant."

"What? What do you mean?"

"Well, it's all a bit risky, isn't it? Bringing in the wife of the deceased for questioning. Accusing her of having an affair with the gardener without any tangible evidence. If it all goes pear-shaped… there will be hell to pay!"

Claire paused. "Hmmm. I hadn't really thought about that until you mentioned it."

"I bet Carter has," said Brian. "So, who's interviewing Mrs Donaldson then?"

"That's what I came over to tell you," Claire replied, smiling at her big colleague "We are!"

Chapter 43

Peter was still sitting in the Dog and Bone, which was considerably busier than it had been in the morning when he had first arrived. He had finished the steak pie and was sipping his third soft drink, and was feeling completely bloated. To make things worse, his bladder was also at the point of bursting but he was reluctant to go to the toilets in case he missed McCafferty leaving the pub.

Another half–hour passed and Peter was now desperate to relieve himself. He decided that he had to take a chance and made a beeline for the toilets. As soon as he was in the back corridor he took a brief look upstairs, listened carefully for any sign of movement and then rushed into the toilets to relieve himself.

A few minutes later, Peter was feeling much better. He quickly washed his hands and dried them on his jacket in the absence of any paper hand towels. Just as he reached for the door, McCafferty pushed the door wide open and entered the toilets. Both men briefly acknowledged each other in passing. Peter noted that McCafferty was wearing a jacket and headed back to the bar. He sat down and kept his eye on the corridor door in the hope that McCafferty would leave the same way he came in—through the front door.

As anticipated, McCafferty entered the bar a few minutes later and spoke to one of the bar staff before leaving. Peter waited until McCafferty reached the front door before moving so it would not be obvious that he was following him.

Once outside, Peter looked left and right and immediately spotted McCafferty heading east on foot. Peter decided to follow him and kept a safe distance. After walking for five minutes, McCafferty turned into what appeared to Peter to be a residential area of the city. The street was lined with rows of red sandstone tenement houses, four or five storeys high on each side, each with an outside door giving access to the close inside, which contained four or five flats on either side of a stone stairwell. Each landing was lit by a small round window—otherwise, the close would be dark during daylight hours.

McCafferty reached his destination and turned into one of the blocks on his right. Peter kept walking past the door McCafferty had entered. He then crossed the road, headed back and stopped in line with the close windows, hoping to see where McCafferty was heading. Peter had no idea if McCafferty was going home or visiting someone but was determined to find out. He thought he saw movement, a change of light in the third-level stairwell window and waited to see if there was any movement on the floor above. *Nothing.*

He decided to take a quick look at the names on the doors of the third floor and prayed that McCafferty was not just dropping in on someone. If McCafferty saw Peter in the corridor he would immediately recognise him as being the man in the pub toilet and would become suspicious. That was the last thing that Peter wanted to happen! He pulled the close door open, quickly entered the block and then let the door shut gently behind him. He stood still for a few seconds and listened for any sign of noise before carefully making his way upstairs. He reached the second level when suddenly he heard a door opening on one of the upper levels. *Shit!*

Peter turned and headed downstairs as fast as he could. He turned right at the bottom of the stairs, hid behind the supporting wall of the stairwell and tried to control his breathing. *Please don't let it be McCafferty,* he prayed to himself. He heard voices getting closer as they descended the stairs; a male and a female, but he couldn't be certain that the male wasn't McCafferty. He heard the front door open and felt the chilly air rush in. His right hand gripped the knife that he had hidden in his pocket in case of any trouble. To his relief the bickering couple left the close, their voices muffled by the closing door and then silence. Although he couldn't be sure, he did not think that the male voice belonged to McCafferty. So, he steadied himself and started to climb the stairs again. This time he managed to reach the third level without incident and checked the names on each door. The first said 'Taylor' and the second 'McCafferty'. *Bingo!*

Happy that he had found McCafferty's home address, Peter made his way downstairs and out of the close. Once outside, he took a deep breath and released it slowly. He marched back to the pub, where he had parked his car and then headed home.

All the way home, he thought about how he would kill McCafferty and more importantly how to do so in a way that would avoid his arrest. It would not be so easy this time; he couldn't use another gas explosion—that would be too much of a coincidence—and besides, innocent people would get hurt in a block of flats. No, he would need to produce something more original and safer than that.

Chapter 44

A nervous-looking Malcolm Munro was sitting in front of DC Jim Armstrong and DC Paul Black in interview room three. The unexpected request for him to return to Dumbarton for further questioning had sent him into a panic and accordingly, he was now desperate and terrified to find out why he had been recalled. He knew McLeish had been interviewed and so he was now worried that he would say something that would contradict McLeish's statement and open up a whole new can of worms, which would end badly for both men. To his relief, the opening question was about Mrs Donaldson and not McLeish.

"So, Mr Munro, how would you describe your relationship with Mrs Donaldson?" asked Jim.

"That's easy, I don't have one."

"According to the Donaldson's cleaner and gardener, you have been at the house on several occasions over the past few weeks. Can you explain why?"

"I was there to see Mr Donaldson on government business," he said confidently, his natural smug disposition slowly returning.

"I see. And what government business would that be?"

"As I explained to DCI…emm, your senior officer, we are working on a number of very important projects at the moment."

Jim looked down at the notes he had been given. "Yes, the new relief road. Is that correct?"

The colour drained from Munro's face at the mention of the road. "Yes, that's one of them."

"I think you stated to DCI *Carter* that it was the most controversial project and that there were many unhappy farmers who would be affected by it."

"Yes, that's correct. DCI Carter was keen to know if anyone could have a possible motive to kill Mr Donaldson."

Jim nodded. "Do you remember speaking to DI Redding about someone called McLeish?"

"Yes, I understand that Mr Donaldson had written a note on a report that she found in his briefcase."

"And you said that you did not know Mr McLeish. Is that correct?" asked Jim.

Munro suddenly became very tense. "Yes."

"That's strange."

"Is it?" replied Munro nervously.

"You see, we were looking through Mr Donaldson's text messages and we found a message from Mr Donaldson to you, which mentions McLeish."

Munro froze. Guilt was written all over his face. "I think I want to speak to a solicitor."

"Why? You are not under arrest, nor are you under caution. We are just asking some questions to clarify Mr Donaldson's relationship with Mr McLeish and *your* relationship with McLeish."

"Nevertheless, I would like to speak to a solicitor. I believe that is my right."

"Of course. We'll get one here as soon as possible. Do you want me to call a duty solicitor or do you have your own?"

"My brother-in-law, Kenneth Williams, is a solicitor. I'll give him a call."

"You do that Mr Munro. Please make yourself comfortable while you are waiting."

Jim and Paul left Munro to make his call and the pair headed back to the incident room to update DI Redding. It was clear that Munro was hiding something and had lied to Claire about knowing McLeish. Thanks to Rambo, they now had the text which proved that Munro must have known McLeish in some capacity, but they knew that it wasn't enough to convict Munro; they would need much more evidence than that to prove that Munro and/or Donaldson had broken any rules, never mind any laws.

When they entered the incident room, Doyle and PC Campbell were sitting at their desks—everyone else had gone.

"Where's the boss?" asked Jim.

"Carter and Rambo are interviewing the gardener and Claire and Brian are in with Mrs Donaldson. You've just missed them. How come you two are back so quickly?" asked Doyle.

"Munro wants a solicitor," Paul replied.

"Really! Sounds like he's got something to hide."

Both Paul and Jim nodded simultaneously. "Without a doubt," replied Jim. "And he definitely lied to the boss about knowing McLeish."

"Definitely something dodgy going on there," said Doyle.

"Yes, but it might not be so easy to prove," said Paul.

The room fell silent as the four men considered Paul's valid comment.

Chapter 45

Ten minutes earlier.

Carly Donaldson and Callum Maclean arrived at the station separately. Both had arranged for a solicitor to be present as they had been warned that they would be interviewed under caution. The pair were directed to their respective interview rooms where the two sets of detectives were waiting. Mrs Donaldson was accompanied by her solicitor, Robert Strange, and sat facing DI Redding and DS O'Neill. In the next room, Callum Maclean was accompanied by his solicitor, George Thomson who sat facing DCI Carter and DS Bahanda. After having been cautioned and had their rights explained to them in full, the interviews began.

Carter began by opening a folder and placing a handful photographs in front of Callum Maclean and his solicitor. "These photographs were taken at the scene of Michael Donaldson's death. According to our forensic team, they are the tyre tracks from a small tractor which we believe was used to haul Mr Donaldson up the tree where he was found hanging." Carter waited to see how Maclean reacted to the information and was disappointed when he received no response.

"Do you own a tractor, Mr Maclean?"

"Yes."

"What type of tractor?"

"It's a John Deere," replied Maclean casually.

"The one with the yellow wheels?" asked Carter.

"Yes, the one with the yellow wheels," Maclean sighed.

"Like this one?" Carter presented another photograph to Maclean and his solicitor.

Maclean picked it up and then passed it to his solicitor. "Yes, like that one."

"For the record, Mr Maclean has confirmed that he owns a John Deere X350R tractor. Mr Maclean, would it surprise you to know that the tracks of this particular make and model of tractor were found at the scene of Mr Donaldson's death?"

"Not really, it's a popular tractor. There must be hundreds of them in use up and down the country."

This was not quite the reaction that Carter was hoping for, so he decided to turn up the heat a little. "For your information, I have requested a warrant to search your property and have instructed a full forensic examination of your tractor. Is there anything you want to share with me before we conduct that search?"

"No, go ahead, I have nothing to hide," said Maclean, again putting Carter on the back foot.

Maclean's solicitor, who had said nothing until that point, decided it was time to intervene. "Chief Inspector, am I correct in thinking that the only reason that my client has been brought in here for questioning today is because he happens to own a similar tractor to one that matches the tracks found near the crime scene? If so, then I think Mr Maclean has answered your questions and it's time to call this interview to a halt."

"Not so fast, Mr Thomson, I'm just getting started. Now, Mr Maclean, did you attend college?"

Thomson intervened again, "I really don't see the relevance of that question."

"All in good time, Mr Thomson, all in good time. Mr Maclean, did you attend college?"

"No, I studied at Glasgow University," said Maclean.

Carter already knew this and persisted with that line of questioning. "And what did you study at university?"

"Botany, I am a gardener," Maclean replied caustically.

"I see. So, you are pretty much an expert on all plants and flowers."

"Well, I have an honours degree but wouldn't necessarily describe myself as an expert."

"Okay, but you admit you have a good knowledge of plants."

"Yes, you could say that."

"And poisonous plants—do you have a good knowledge of those?"

For the first time, Maclean hesitated, and both detectives saw it. "Some."

"Ever heard of viscumin?" asked Carter.

"No. I don't think I have."

Carter didn't expect Maclean to admit to that piece of knowledge—that would have been too much to hope for, but his hesitation on the previous question was enough to confirm to Carter that Maclean had lied to him. "Really? You studied botany at university and you expect me to believe that you have no knowledge of a poison found in something as common as mistletoe?"

Thomson raised his hand to stop Maclean from responding to the question. "Chief Inspector, I believe my client has answered your question. It doesn't matter what you believe or not, it only matters what you can prove, and that appears to be very little in this case, so if there's nothing further…"

Carter ignored the solicitor and decided to increase the pressure. "Mr Maclean, what is your relationship with Mrs Donaldson?"

~

Claire and Brian sat facing Carly Donaldson and her solicitor, Robert Strange. It was clear from her disposition that Mrs

Donaldson was far from happy and did not want to be there.

Strange spoke first. "Inspector, before you commence questioning my client, I would like you to know that she is extremely upset and disappointed that she is being treated like a suspect. Her husband has just been killed and you have done nothing but harass her, which I think is appalling. I understand that this is the third time she has been interviewed, and so far, there has been no evidence of any kind to suggest that she was involved. That being the case, I think you should know that I intend to submit a formal complaint about your behaviour to your superiors as soon as this interview is over."

If Brian was feeling uncomfortable before the interview, he was feeling much worse now. However, the solicitor's threat did not appear to have any effect on Claire, who simply smiled at Strange and proceeded to ask her questions as if nothing of importance had been said.

"Mrs Donaldson, we now know that your husband was poisoned before he was hanged, and we suspect that he was taken from your home and that a small tractor was used to haul him up the tree. However, what I am struggling to understand, assuming that's what happened, is how did your husband's killer get access to your house to poison him without having to break in? There was no sign of forced entry, no sign of a struggle." Claire paused to allow Mrs Donaldson to absorb this information "Who, other than you and your husband, has keys to your property?"

"My cleaner, Mrs Muldoon, and my gardener—Callum."

"And no one else has access?"

"No, why do you ask?"

"Well, I thought it would be obvious. If no one else has the keys then either you, or Mrs Muldoon, or Mr Maclean poisoned your husband—or at the very least allowed the killer to enter the house." Claire knew that this was a bit of a stretch, but it was all she had to work with. She paused for a moment to see if there was any reaction. There was nothing, which was a little disconcerting, so she continued.

"Mrs Muldoon has provided a solid alibi which has been confirmed by her husband so that leaves you and Mr Maclean as the main suspects." Claire paused again to see if there was any reaction. Again there was nothing so Claire pushed on. "Mrs Donaldson, what is your relationship with Callum Maclean?"

"Don't answer that," said Strange. "This is all supposition, Inspector. You have not presented a single shred of evidence that links my client to this crime. It's preposterous."

Claire ignored Strange and pressed on with the next question, hoping to catch her out. "Do you own a tractor, Mrs Donaldson?"

"What? No, no I don't."

"Does your gardener, Mr Maclean, own a tractor?"

"Yes, he uses it to cut the grass. We have a huge lawn, as you know."

"Yes, and can you describe this tractor?"

"I think it's green, with yellow wheels."

Claire removed a photograph of the John Deere tractor from her folder and passed it to Mrs Donaldson. "Is that the one?"

"Yes, it certainly looks like it."

"Mrs Donaldson. I'm going to ask this question again and I would appreciate a straight answer. What is your relationship with Callum Maclean?"

There was a look of sudden realisation on Carly Donaldson's face, and then her concern turned into a smile and she started to laugh. Both Claire and Brian were perplexed by this change of behaviour.

"Oh no, Inspector, I think you've made a huge mistake."

"What do you mean?"

"You think that Callum and I are having an affair and planned to kill Mike, don't you? That's hilarious." She burst out laughing again, much to Claire's annoyance.

"I don't think this is a laughing matter, Mrs Donaldson," said Claire, doing her best to suppress her anger.

"But it is, Inspector. You see, Callum Maclean is gay!"

~

"I'm her gardener," replied Maclean.

"Yes, but you're friendly. You chat a lot… yes?" prompted Carter.

"Yes, as I've said before—we talk about plants for the garden."

"What about Mr Donaldson? Did you talk to him about the garden?" asked Carter.

Before Maclean could respond, there was a knock at the door and DI Redding appeared. "Sorry boss, could I have a word? Something important has come up."

If Carter was annoyed at the interruption, he didn't show it. He checked his watch. "Interview suspended at 2.20 p.m., Detective Chief Inspector Carter leaving the room." Rambo stopped the recording and remained seated.

Carter stepped outside the room. "What have you got?"

"I got it all wrong. It turns out Callum Maclean is gay!"

"What!"

"Carly Donaldson has just confirmed it, so they couldn't have been having an affair. She's in there laughing her head off!"

"Shit!"

"Yes but think about it. It doesn't mean that Maclean is innocent—it just means we have nothing to connect Mrs Donaldson and Maclean..." Claire stopped dead in her tracks. "Of course..."

"Of course what, Claire?" asked Carter.

"It just occurred to me that Maclean knew David Donaldson. They went to school together—Maclean mentioned this in his first interview."

Carter nodded. "And David Donaldson told us that he was gay! Right then, let's get him in for further questioning."

"What about Mrs Donaldson?" asked Claire.

"We'll have to let her go."

"Shit! We're going to get a complaint about harassment. Her solicitor made such a big deal about it, and now that we've got this all wrong…"

"Don't worry about it—the Chief Super won't care about a petty complaint if we nail the actual killer. So, your priority is David Donaldson—find him and bring him in. I'll continue pushing Maclean now that we know that he's gay and see what happens. He's been a smug git up until now, and no wonder—he knew where I was going with Mrs Donaldson and he was more than happy for me to continue down that road. Okay, once you're finished with Mrs Donaldson, find out if the search warrant has come through—I want his house searched from top to bottom and his tractor brought in for a thorough forensic examination. We need to find one piece of hard evidence and we'll have him."

"Yes, boss. I'll get onto it right away." Claire turned and returned to interview room one, where she would need to eat humble pie and let Mrs Donaldson leave. She hated admitting that she was wrong, but worse still, she would have to do so in front of Robert Strange, LLB, the most arrogant and obnoxious of all the local solicitors.

Chapter 46

Claire entered the incident room and immediately noticed that Jim and Paul were sitting there.

"Have you two finished with Munro?" she asked.

"Not quite, boss," said Paul. "He's asked for a solicitor."

"How far did you get?"

"As soon as we mentioned the relief road, he got nervous but it wasn't until we told him about the text message that he insisted on seeing his solicitor," replied Paul.

Claire grinned. "He is definitely up to something if he thinks he needs a solicitor. Caution him in front of the solicitor, ask all the same questions over again. Give him the chance to trip himself up or change his story, then keep pushing him and see what happens."

"We will, boss. How did you get on with the wife?" asked Jim.

"Not so good. We've had to let Mrs Donaldson go—it turns out the gardener is gay, so he couldn't have been having an affair with her."

"You're kidding! So what now?"

"Well, the DCI is convinced that the gardener's involved, so he's in there with him now asking about his relationship with David Donaldson."

"Who? The brother?" asked Paul.

"Yes, and Brian and I are going to bring him in for questioning. After all, he has the greatest motive for murder."

"But I thought you and Carter were convinced he was innocent."

"Thanks for reminding me!" said Claire. She turned towards Brian who had just hung up the phone. "Any joy?"

"Nope. No answer, he must be at work."

"Could be," said Claire, checking her watch. "Keep trying."

One of the landline phones rang and everyone looked at Paul, who was nearest. He read the signal, got up and picked up the receiver. "CID. Oh, hi Sarge. Thanks, bring him up to interview room three." He turned and shouted over to Jim. "That's Munro's solicitor arrived. Let's go."

~

Carter returned to the interview room and nodded to Rambo, who turned on the recording device and stated who was in the room, again.

"So, Mr Maclean, where were we? Ah yes, I was asking you about Mr Michael Donaldson. What was your relationship with Mr Donaldson?"

"I didn't have one."

"Did you like him?"

"Not particularly."

"Oh! Why was that?

"No particular reason."

"And what about David Donaldson?" asked Carter.

For the first time, Maclean was notably shaken. "What about him?"

"Do you like him?" asked Carter

Maclean didn't respond. Instead, he whispered something to his solicitor, who in turn whispered back to him. "No comment," said Maclean.

Carter smiled. "Are you having an affair with Mr David Donaldson?"

"No comment."

"When was the last time you spoke with David Donaldson?"

"No comment."

"Did you and David Donaldson plot to kill his brother?"

"No."

Carter paused. He knew there was no point continuing with the interview now that the 'no comment' routine had been triggered. However, he was now convinced of Maclean's guilt and wasn't prepared to release him, not yet. He looked at Thomson. "Mr Maclean will remain in custody while we carry out further investigations. As you know, I can hold him for up to twelve hours and could request an extension up to a maximum of twenty-four hours, if deemed necessary. I'm sure you will want to explain the rules of custody with your client in private, so we will leave you to do so. In the meantime, this interview is suspended."

Rambo turned off the recorder and both detectives left the room. As soon as the door closed, Carter checked his phone and saw a text from Claire confirming that the search warrant had come through. He turned to Rambo. "Wait here until the solicitor leaves and then take Maclean downstairs to the custody sergeant."

"Will do, boss."

Carter turned and headed towards the incident room. The clock was ticking!

Chapter 47

Carter burst into the incident room and made a beeline for Claire. "Any news on David Donaldson?"

"Nope. Brian's been calling his mobile every fifteen minutes and getting no reply. He might be working."

"Or on the run," said Carter. He looked around the office and made up his mind. "Right, I'm going to search Maclean's house. Doyle, Campbell—you're coming with me. Call the SOC Team and get one of their officers to assist us. Preferably somebody senior.

Doyle immediately picked up the phone and made the call.

Carter turned back to Claire. "Rambo's taking Maclean down into custody so we need to move fast. You and Brian go to the brother's house. By all means keep calling him, but if you get no response, knock on doors and find out when he was last seen by his neighbours. I want him here while I still have Maclean in custody."

"So, you still think Maclean is guilty."

"Oh yes, there was a definite reaction when we asked him about David Donaldson."

"Right. Brian and I will get going. Someone let Rambo know that he's in charge while we are all out."

"Why? Where's Jim and Paul?"

"Still in with Munro. He insisted on getting a solicitor."

"Good. I knew he was at it. Okay, I'll get someone to tell Rambo while we're waiting for confirmation of the SOCO. You two get going and keep in touch."

~

By the time Claire and Brian arrived at David Donaldson's flat, Claire was convinced that Carter was right and that Donaldson was on the run. She had called his number every five minutes and got nothing other than his voicemail message.

They entered the block of flats and headed straight for Donaldson's house, hoping that he was there and that there was some reasonable explanation as to why he wasn't answering his mobile. Brian knocked on the door loudly, rang the doorbell and then stood back. He waited for about five seconds and tried again. Nothing.

"Are you looking for David?" a voice said from behind them.

Brian and Claire turned to see who had just spoken. "Yes," said Claire, smiling at the elderly woman, who was about to enter her flat next to Donaldson's. "Have you seen him today?"

"Yes, about an hour ago. He was pulling a small case."

"A case?" asked Brian.

"Yes, you know—the type of case some people take on board a plane with them. I assumed he was going away for the weekend."

"Right. Did he say where he was going?" asked Claire.

"No dear, I only saw him from my window. He seemed like he was in a hurry, though."

"Right. Thank you. You've been extremely helpful."

"He's not in any trouble, is he?"

"No, we just want to ask him a few questions, that's all," said Claire.

"So, you are the police?"

"Yes, sorry. We should have identified ourselves. I'm Detective Claire Redding and this is Detective Sergeant Brian O'Neill."

"Oh, that's a relief. You know, David is a lovely young man. Always offering to help me with my shopping and take the bins out."

"I'm sure he is. I'm sorry, we're going to have to go now. Thank you for your help."

Claire and Brian made their way out of the building and back to their car. "To the airport?" asked Brian.

"Yes, as fast as you can. I'll call it in and get Rambo to check with the airport to see if he's booked onto any flights. Hopefully, the plane won't have left before we get there."

"What if he's getting the bus and not a flight?"

"Well if he did, and I can't think why, I'd be less worried. It'll take him a lot longer to get out of the country on a bus! Assuming he's actually on the run!"

"True. But it looks a bit suspicious though. I wonder if Maclean called him from the station."

"Who knows? Right, let's get going. The game is afoot!"

"What is it with you and Sherlock Holmes?" asked Brian.

"Shoosh! While I speak to Rambo. I'll explain on the way."

The car headed towards the motorway, blue lights flashing and siren wailing at the cars in front to get out of the way, but the busy Glasgow traffic did its best to slow their progress.

Chapter 48

Carter entered Maclean's house armed with a set of keys that Maclean had willingly handed over on sight of the search warrant. He opened the front door to allow the search party to enter and then made a beeline to the garage at the back of the property where Maclean had told him the tractor would be found. He opened the heavy padlock on the garage door and slid back the rusty bolt. Once inside, he found the light switch and turned on the lights. The tractor was sitting in the middle of the garage. It looked exceptionally clean. It was obvious to Carter that Maclean had cleaned it—there was no sign of any dirt from the field or anywhere else for that matter. *Shit!* Carter went back outside and found the SOCO.

"I want that tractor taken in and examined inch by inch. It looks like the bastard's jet-washed it. Take it to pieces if you must, but I need it done pronto. I have the suspect in custody and the clock's ticking."

The SOCO looked in shock. "Right, but it might take some time…"

"Listen, sunshine, I've just explained. I've not got time, so get it done pronto – or do you want me to speak to your boss?"

"Yes sir. I mean no, sir. I mean… I'll call in a recovery vehicle and take it back to the depot for examination A.S.A.P. I'll call for more assistance—I thought I was only here to take a sample of mud from the wheels."

"Aye, me too, son," said Carter, looking around the rest of the grounds.

The SOCO started to make the call while Carter returned to the garage to complete his search. Having found nothing else of interest, he moved on to the greenhouse at the back of the garden and could see what appeared to be some sort of homemade chemistry set comprising glass beakers, a Bunsen burner attached to a small bottle of Calor gas and various jars full of white powder. Some were marked 'poison.' Carter went looking for the SOCO, who had just finished his call and summoned him over to the greenhouse. He instructed the SOCO to take photographs and then bag all of the equipment and jars for further analysis.

Carter returned to the house to see if his team had found anything else of interest, but there was nothing more to be found. He checked his phone and could see a message from Rambo confirming Donaldson was at the airport and that Claire and Brian were on their way. *Looks like I was right—he's on the run.* He called Rambo to let him know that he was on his way back to the station.

Chapter 49

Claire and Brian arrived at Glasgow Airport and abandoned their car outside the main entrance to Terminal 1. They had been told that Donaldson was somewhere in the departure lounge (he had checked in and passed through security before the alert had been issued). So far, the armed police on duty at the airport had been unable to identify him from the description given, which was not surprising as it was so vague it could have fitted half the male population of Scotland.

The two detectives made a beeline to the information desk on the ground floor and were immediately directed to the UK Departure Gate 7. According to the airport booking system, Donaldson was booked on a flight to Heathrow that was now embarking. Claire and Brian sprinted to the escalator and bounded up the moving stairs as quickly as they could. Claire headed for the priority entry gate at the security checkpoint and turned to see if Brian was following her. Brian was folded over at the top of the escalator, desperately trying to catch his breath. He waved at Claire to go on, which she did. She held up her ID and shouted 'Police' to the security officer, who immediately let her through without properly checking her ID. She then sprinted through the scanners, again displaying her badge and shouting 'Police' at the top of her voice. Even Claire was feeling a bit breathless by the time she reached the duty-free section. She stopped briefly to see if Brian was following her but couldn't see him, so she continued to run into the departure lounge and through the entrance to the UK departure gates. She looked up and saw the sign for Gate 7 and jogged towards the gate, unable to sustain her earlier sprint. *I really need to get into shape*, she thought.

When she arrived, she saw a queue of passengers boarding Gate 7. She moved along the line checking for Donaldson but he wasn't there, so she approached the desk and once again held up her ID. "DI Redding, Police Scotland. Has David Donaldson gone through?" she puffed, trying to catch her breath. It only took the flight attendant a few seconds to confirm that he had and Claire was on the move again, this time leaping downstairs two at a time towards the gate and then outside to the area where the British Airways aeroplane was being boarded. There were two flights of stairs being used to board passengers, and Claire headed straight for the nearest set at the front of the plane. When she arrived inside the cabin, she was greeted by one of the cabin crew.

"Good afternoon. Please take your seat as quickly as possible."

Claire raised her ID. "Police, I need to speak to one of your passengers. A Mr David Donaldson."

"Oh, right. Hold on, I'll call him forward." She picked up the phone next to her and invited Mr David Donaldson to come forward. She repeated the message over the loudspeaker.

Claire could see movement in the middle of the plane as Donaldson made his way slowly to the front. The look of surprise on his face when he saw who was waiting for him was evident for all to see. Finally, he managed to squeeze by the last passenger in the aisle and approached the detective. "What's this all about?" he asked.

"David Donaldson, you are under arrest on suspicion of murder." There was the sound of gasps from some of the passengers at the front of the plane as they reacted to what they had just heard. Claire ignored this and continued to caution Donaldson, whose expression was more shock than surprise.

"I don't understand, I haven't done anything," he pleaded.

"Do you have any luggage?"

"Yes, a small case. It's back there above my seat."

"Okay, I'll come with you and you can retrieve it." Claire turned to the stewardess, who also appeared to be in a state of shock. "Can you hold back these passengers until we get his case?"

"Yes, of course."

Claire followed Donaldson back to his seat and could see that the other passengers were all rather excited to witness the arrest of a murderer. He pulled the small case down and followed Claire back to the front of the plane, where there was now a considerable number of passengers waiting to be seated. Claire and

Donaldson stood aside to allow them to pass before making their way back down the stairs towards the terminal. At the foot of the stairs, Claire decided to handcuff Donaldson. However, instead of handcuffing his hands together behind him, she decided to do it at the front as he would need to climb the stairs unassisted. She picked up his case and directed him back to the terminal. She wondered what had happened to Brian. *Had he gotten lost?* She made her way back to the security area, where a large crowd of people had gathered. She soon realised that someone was on the floor and there were paramedics around him. "Brian! Oh no!"

Claire pushed Donaldson through the crowd and reached the paramedics. "Is he alright?"

"Are you family?" asked one of the paramedics instinctively. He hadn't noticed Claire was holding onto a man in handcuffs."

"No, I'm a police officer and he's my colleague—Sergeant Brian O'Neill."

"Oh, right. Well, it looks like it was a heart attack. He wasn't breathing when we arrived but we used the AED to shock him and we now have a weak pulse. We'll give him some more oxygen and move him when he's a bit more stable."

"Thank God for that," said Claire. Brian was not looking well at all. His skin had a blue-grey tinge and looked very clammy.

"Do you want to come to the hospital with him?" asked the other paramedic.

"No, I need to take this man to the station, but I'll call his wife, Agnes, and let her know. Where are you taking him?"

"The Queen Elizabeth is the nearest."

Claire steeled herself and made the call to Agnes. Shen called Rambo and told him about Brian and that she was bringing in Donaldson. Finally, she called Peter to let him know about Brian and that she was going to be working late again. She bent down and put her hand on Brian's forehead. He was still unconscious, but was breathing easier than before. "You hold on there, you big lummox!" A small tear ran down her cheek which she wiped away with her sleeve. She rummaged through Brian's jacket pocket and found the car keys and then stood up and turned to Donaldson. "Come on, we need to get you back to the station."

"I'm sorry," he said, which caught Claire off-guard.

"What?"

"About your colleague."

"Oh, I see. Yes, so am I, come on."

She picked up his case, led him down to the car and placed him carefully in the back seat. The journey back to Dumbarton was a quiet one. Donaldson had decided to take the caution seriously and said nothing—he would wait until his solicitor showed up before speaking again.

Claire was absorbed in her own thoughts about Brian and then about Donaldson. His behaviour since his arrest was bothering her. Firstly, he didn't try to escape and secondly, there was genuine surprise on his face when he saw her on the plane. She had been convinced that he was on the run when Rambo had confirmed he had checked in at the airport, but now… not so much.

Chapter 50

Claire's message to Peter was all he needed to convince himself that now was the time to take care of McCafferty. She was working late again, and who knew when the next opportunity would present itself. He had also come up with a plan to disable McCafferty and get entry to his flat.

He packed his backpack with everything he needed: knife, tape, balaclava, rope and most importantly Claire's police-issued pepper spray, which she kept in the bottom of her cupboard. He had accidentally stumbled upon it when looking for gloves and was delighted to find it was still there when he went back to look.

Peter finished packing and went downstairs, where Sally was waiting patiently for her evening walk. He looked at his wee dog and decided that it would only be fair to walk her before he went out. He picked up the lead and shouted for Sally to come over. He bent down, hooking the lead onto her collar, and made his way out of the house and onto the cycle path. He loved the area where he lived, particularly the cycle path where he had first seen Claire jogging. Every time he walked Sally, he would remember seeing Claire for the first time and thinking that he should ask her out. And had it not been for Sally tripping Claire up outside of Asda, he might never have worked up the courage to speak to her, never mind ask her out. Things hadn't been so good with Claire since her accident and he blamed Petrie and his men for that, but tonight he would put an end to all of that and hopefully, he and Claire could start to rebuild their relationship again.

~

Claire arrived back in the station and took Donaldson to the custody desk, where he would be booked in and held in a cell until his solicitor arrived. Claire headed upstairs to the incident room and immediately asked Rambo for an update on Brian.

"He's okay. They have him at the Queen Elizabeth, under observation."

"Thank God for that," said Claire. "I'll pop in and see how he's doing later." She looked around the room. "Where's Carter?"

"He's with the Chief, giving an update on our progress. Shouldn't be too long."

"What about the search? Anything?"

"Yeah, they found a whole load of chemistry gear in his greenhouse and took it down to the lab for analysis."

"And the tractor. Anything?"

"Oh yes, they found the tractor, but it had been power-washed," replied Rambo, who mimicked the actions of the power-hose but looked more like he was using a machine gun.

Claire shook her head in bemusement. "I see, so what did Carter do about it?"

"The usual… he went ballistic and instructed the SOCO to take it apart. He's determined to find something while he still has Maclean in custody. I dare say he is speaking to the Chief about an extension."

"I bet he is," said Claire. "It could take forensics a while to find anything."

"Yeah, he even sent Doyle down there to make sure they keep on it."

"Blimey, he is serious. Where's Jim and Paul?"

"On a break. The boss wants them back to assist with the interviews. He wants to double up again, and he wants Maclean to know that we have Donaldson in custody. Is he being held downstairs?"

"Yes, I'll bring him up when the solicitor gets here."

"Perfect. We can time it so Maclean sees Donaldson," said Rambo. "The boss will be pleased."

"Sounds like a plan. Right, I'm heading up to the canteen to get a quick sandwich while I can. Give me a shout when the solicitor gets here."

"No problem."

~

Peter arrived on foot outside McCafferty's block. He had parked his car a few streets away just to be safe. He looked up at the third floor and could see lights on in McCafferty's flat. He waited for a few moments and then saw movement, a shadow against the closed blinds. He was in luck. He entered the close, closed the outer door and waited to hear if anyone was coming down the stairs. *Nothing*. He made his way up to the third floor. He took out his balaclava and pulled it over his face. He then took out the pepper spray and put his finger on the aerosol release at the top to make sure it was working. A small puff of spray was released and he was satisfied that he was ready. He took a deep breath to steady himself and knocked loudly on the door. He heard footsteps approach the door and stood to the side. He heard the lock turn and, to his surprise, a woman's voice. "Is that you Danny?"

Peter grabbed his balaclava and shoved it in his pocket just as the old woman appeared. "Hello, I'm looking for Danny. I take it he's not here," said Peter.

The woman looked up at Peter, who attempted to put on his most pleasant and least threatening face. "No son, he's no' here."

"But he does live here?" asked Peter, pointing to the nameplate.

"Naw, I'm his maw. He's no' lived here for years."

"Ah right. Sorry. Could you tell me where he lives now?"

"Who did you say you were, again?"

Peter decided to take a chance. "I'm an old friend. We used to work in the pub together. My name is Bob, Bob Wilson. I was in Glasgow and thought I'd drop in and see Danny."

Peter waited to see if she had bought his story; she seemed very sharp for her age. She smiled at Peter for the first time. "You know, come to think of it, I think Danny has mentioned working with someone called Bob before."

"That would be me," said Peter grinning.

"Danny's over in the new housing estate at East Mearns. Lovely big house. He's doing really well for himself," she said.

I bet he is, thought Peter. "Do you have his address?"

"Oh, aye. It's, eh, East Mearns Grove. Now, whit number wiz it again? Oh, aye, I remember now. It's fifty-four."

"Fifty–four, East Mearns Grove," Peter repeated. "Thanks, that's great. You've been extremely helpful, Mrs McCafferty."

"No bother son. I'll give Danny a call and let him know you're coming."

"Oh! No need to do that and besides, I'd prefer to surprise him. He's not seen me for years."

The woman stared up at Peter and grinned. "Okay son, suit yourself but I should warn you… our Danny doesn't like surprises!" She closed the door and left Peter standing there. He kicked himself for being so careless, but at least he now had the correct address. He googled it and saw it was only ten minutes away by car. He made up his mind to go there and get it over with. After all, McCafferty's mother knew he would be at home—she was about to phone him there before Peter stopped her. He quickly made his way to his car and headed off towards East Mearns.

Chapter 51

Carly Donaldson's and Callum Maclean's solicitors arrived at the station within five minutes of each other and were now waiting for their clients in separate interview rooms. It had been agreed that Claire and Jim would interview Donaldson while Carter and Paul would try to break Maclean. Carter and Claire went down to the cells to collect their respective prisoners, as had been planned. Claire instructed the custody sergeant to open Donaldson's cell first. He did so, entered the cell and told Donaldson to turn around so he could handcuff his hands behind his back. He then led him into the cell corridor where Claire was waiting.

"Just wait there, Mr Donaldson. Your solicitor has arrived, and I'll take you up to see him in a few moments," Claire explained.

Carter instructed the custody sergeant to open Maclean's cell and then stood back to allow Maclean to enter the corridor. As soon as he saw Donaldson standing there, the colour drained from his face. This was the reaction that Carter had been hoping for.

"David!" Maclean exclaimed.

Donaldson turned instantly, recognising the voice. "Callum?"

Maclean turned to Carter. "What's the meaning of this? What's he doing here?"

Carter grinned. "Let's go upstairs and find out, shall we?"

Claire led Donaldson up to the CID corridor and Carter followed with Maclean, who was clearly agitated at the sight of Donaldson. Donaldson, meanwhile, appeared to be genuinely confused by the whole scenario.

Once inside interview room two, Claire removed his handcuffs. "I'll give you a few minutes to speak to your solicitor before we begin." She stepped outside and could see Carter and Maclean enter the room next to hers. Paul and Jim made their way along the corridor and for the first time during the investigation, Paul looked excited. He had a few sheets of paper in his hand and waved them at Claire. "I've just received the initial forensics on the tractor."

~

East Mearns housing estate was like every other new private housing estate that Peter had seen – rows and rows of perfect square boxes with pristine lawns, red brick driveways, white-doored garages and absolutely no character whatsoever. Peter much preferred his old red sandstone house, built in the 1920s with high ceilings and spacious rooms, albeit the large bay window could be a bit draughty at times.

He followed his sat nav's directions and turned into East Mearns Grove, driving slowly until he reached number fifty-four. He then drove on and parked further up the street, where there were a few empty public parking spaces in a small bay. He sat for a few moments thinking about how to approach McCafferty. *What could he say that would at least get him into the hallway?* He quickly made up his mind and headed back toward number fifty-four, determined to finish what he had started.

~

DC Armstrong switched on the recording device and camera, and Claire repeated the caution that she had previously given Donaldson at the airport. She stated who was in the room and then proceeded with the interview. Donaldson's solicitor, John Hutchinson, took out his yellow legal notepad and said nothing – the opposite of Robert Strange.

Claire commenced the interview. "Mr Donaldson, when DCI Carter and I interviewed you at your home, you stated that you hated your brother, Michael Donaldson, but did not kill him? Is that still your position?"

"Yes."

"And at that time, you also stated that you were a homosexual. Is that correct?"

"Inspector, I really don't see the relevance of that question," said Hutchinson.

Claire put her hand up to stop the solicitor from saying any more. "A few more questions and all will become crystal clear. Mr Donaldson, what is your relationship with Callum Maclean?"

Before Hutchinson could stop his client from answering, Donaldson responded quite openly, "We were lovers."

Hutchinson wrote a note on his pad and showed it to Donaldson. It said: 'Don't say anything else.'

Claire continued. "Were lovers? You are no longer in that relationship?"

"No, it ended a long time ago," Donaldson replied, deliberately ignoring the advice of his solicitor.

This was not the response that Claire was hoping for, but she pushed on as if everything were fine. "When did it end and may I ask, why?"

Donaldson looked a little deflated. "It was just after I told my family that I was gay. As you know, they didn't react very well, and when I told them that Callum and I were an item, they went ballistic. They blamed Callum for turning me - as if that were possible! Worse still, Michael told Callum that unless he ended the affair, his father's business would be finished—he even threatened to speak to all of our neighbours and make sure of it. It broke Callum's heart to end our relationship, but he couldn't risk his father's business - his father had built up that business over many years, and Callum knew it would destroy him if it collapsed. I couldn't stay there after that; it was too painful, so I left home and got a flat in Glasgow."

"I see. So, when was the last time you spoke to Callum Maclean?" asked Claire.

"A few weeks ago. I bumped into him in the town."

"In Glasgow," Claire clarified.

"Yes, sorry Glasgow."

"What did you talk about?"

"Oh, this and that. You know, just catching up."

"And how was he? Was he happy to see you?"

"Yes, yes he was, but there was a sadness about him."

"And did you talk about Michael?"

Hutchinson, sensing a trap, tapped his pen on the message on the legal pad, but Donaldson ignored him. "Yes, he wasn't happy when I told him about Mike taking my share of the inheritance. In fact, he was pretty angry… hold on, you don't think Callum killed Mike… do you? Is that why you have him here? Oh God, no!"

"Mr Donaldson, I'm afraid I have to tell you that we have found substantial evidence that links Callum Maclean to the murder of your brother and…"

"Inspector, before you continue, I would like a few minutes in private with my client, if you don't mind."

Claire rolled her eyes at Hutchinson, "Very well, interview suspended at 18:15."

~

Maclean's initial agitation at seeing Donaldson had continued into the interview room, where he was now being questioned by Carter for the second time that day. "Mr Maclean, we have conducted a search of your home and have found several items of interest which we would like you to explain."

"Before I say anything, I want to know why David is here," he demanded.

"We will come to that, but before we do, I want to show you some photographs taken at your house." Carter pushed photographs of the makeshift chemistry set that he had found in the greenhouse in front of Maclean. "Can you explain why you have this equipment in your greenhouse?"

Maclean glanced at the photographs. "I use it to make up my own special mix of weedkiller. I use a lot of the stuff and find it's much cheaper to make up my own formulae instead of buying in an expensive brand."

Carter had to admit that it was a good answer. "Right, and you would use a Bunsen burner to do that?"

"Yes, some of the ingredients need a bit of heat and water to mix together properly."

"And you learned to do this while studying botany?" asked Carter.

"Among other things, yes," Maclean replied.

Carter picked up the sheet of paper that Paul had handed to him at the start of the interview. "We also found something interesting when examining your tractor, Mr Maclean," said Carter, who then paused for maximum effect. "According to the forensic report which I have just been handed, particles of glass were found embedded in the tyres of your tractor." Again, he paused, this time looking at Maclean's face for a reaction.

Maclean kept a poker face and replied quite pointedly, "That's not unusual, is it? I must have gone over lots of glass in the course of my work."

Carter nodded as if agreeing with Maclean. "Yes, but what is special about this particular glass is that it matches glass that our forensic team found at the scene of the crime. You see, our clever little scientists examined the structure of the glass in detail and are 99.9% certain that they have matched the glass found on your vehicle with samples taken at the scene. That puts your tractor at the scene of the crime. Care to explain what you were doing with your tractor in that field?"

Maclean looked sick. "No comment."

"Surprise, surprise! Well, let me tell you what I think happened. You and David Donaldson plotted to kill his brother. You poisoned him and…"

"What? No, you're wrong. David has nothing to do with …" said Maclean, who stopped himself but knew it was too late.

"Had nothing to do with what?" prompted Carter. "The murder of his brother? The same brother who stole his inheritance! You honestly expect me to believe that David is innocent? Oh come on Callum, you can't expect me to believe that. No, you are both going down for this!"

Maclean sprang out of his seat in a complete rage. "Leave him alone, he's innocent. I did it. I did it all! I hated that bastard. What he did to David. What he did to us! Well, I showed him, didn't I…"

Carter smiled at Maclean. "Sit down, Mr Maclean."

Maclean flopped back down into the seat, a defeated man.

"Okay, why don't you tell us how you did it… all on your own," said Carter sarcastically. As Maclean started to tell his story, Carter wondered how Claire was getting on with David Donaldson.

~

Claire and Jim returned to the interview room, ready to have another go at Donaldson. Jim turned on the recorder and Claire recommenced the interview. During the break, she had decided to take a different approach in the hope that Donaldson would crumble under pressure.

"Mr Donaldson please explain why you tried to leave the country when DCI Carter specifically asked you not to do so?" asked Claire.

Donaldson turned to his solicitor, who nodded his approval to proceed. "I wasn't leaving the country; I was going to London."

"Mr Donaldson, I think you'll find that Scotland is a country. It has its own Parliament; it makes its own laws and has its own Police force."

"Yes, but I thought he meant the UK."

Claire rolled her eyes. "Okay. So, why were you going to London?"

Again, Donaldson turned to his solicitor, who nodded his consent to continue.

"To visit a friend."

"A friend?"

"Yes, an old University pal. Fred Wiseman. He's an accountant now and has a flat in the east end. You can check with him if you want. In fact, you'll do me a favour as he'll be wondering where I am. My flight should have landed by now. I can give you his mobile."

"That would be helpful," said Claire, acutely aware that she had nothing on Donaldson if his friend confirmed his story.

She took down the details of the mobile number and continued. "When did you make the arrangements to see your friend?"

"A week ago. We've been talking about this visit for weeks, but I couldn't find a gap in my diary until now."

"And he will be able to confirm that?" asked Claire.

There was a knock on the door and DCI Carter popped his head into the room. "Claire, can I have a word?"

She suspended the interview and left the room.

Carter was grinning. "Maclean has confessed and his story matched the evidence, but I'm still not clear if Donaldson was involved or not. Maclean says not – do you have anything?"

Claire shook her head. "Nothing, he was genuinely shocked at the suggestion that Maclean had killed Michael, and I'm just about to check his reason for attempting to leave the country."

"Okay, do it quickly. I'm about to speak to the Fiscal about pressing charges on Maclean and I need to know if Donaldson is in the clear or not."

"Right, I'll do it now."

Claire made the call and spoke to a very anxious and concerned Fred Wiseman, who had been told by the airline that David Donaldson had been removed from the plane by the police. He then went on to confirm everything Donaldson had said.

Claire hung up her phone and looked at Carter. "Donaldson's in the clear. We have nothing on him."

"Right. Let him go and tell him we'll cover the cost of his missed flight. That should prevent another complaint."

"Another one?"

"Yeah, that prick Strange has written to the Chief about you."

"Great! That's all I need."

"Don't worry. I'll be sure to tell the Chief that I couldn't have solved this one without you."

"Yeah, well. I've made a few mistakes along the way."

"We both have, Claire. Don't beat yourself up over it. We've got the killer under lock and key. That's all that really matters."

"Yeah, but if I hadn't gone chasing after Donaldson at the airport then Brian wouldn't be in hospital, would he?"

"You don't know that; his heart attack could have happened at any time. Anyway, the big man is doing okay, isn't he?"

Claire nodded. "I'm going to see him as soon as we're done here."

"Good, so let's get back in there and take care of business."

They turned simultaneously and entered the interview rooms.

Chapter 52

Peter strolled casually towards McCafferty's door. He looked up and down the street to check if anyone was looking, decided it was safe and rang the bell.

Danny McCafferty was sitting in his kitchen having a beer. His ready meal of choice—spaghetti bolognaise—was in the oven and would be ready to eat in five minutes, according to the clock at the top of the electric oven. Needless to say, he was less than amused when the doorbell rang. *Who the fuck is that at this time of night?* He waddled through to the hall with a beer bottle in one hand and opened the door with the other.

"Can I help you?" he growled at the man dressed in black.

"Baxter sent me," said Peter. He knew that would get McCafferty's attention.

"What! Why?"

"Not out here," said Peter, looking around surreptitiously.

"Do I know you from somewhere?" said McCafferty, scanning Peter's face.

"Maybe from the pub. I drink there sometimes."

That sparked a memory. "Aye, that's right, you better come in then."

"What does Baxter want?" asked McCafferty standing back to allow Peter to enter the narrow hallway.

Peter stepped inside and closed the door behind him. He felt the small bottle of pepper spray in his hand which he had kept hidden in his right-hand pocket.

"To give you a message."

Peter pulled his hand out of his jacket pocket and sprayed McCafferty directly in his eyes. McCafferty staggered back, screaming and cursing, wiping his eyes desperately with his sleeve, trying and failing to relieve the burning pain. Peter tried to grab hold of him, but McCafferty resisted and swung at Peter, catching his forehead with the hard bottom edge of the bottle. Peter shouted in agony and jumped back from McCafferty, who was now swinging the bottle blindly in all directions.

Peter touched his head which now had a nasty gash and was bleeding. *Shit.* Anger and fear overtook him and he charged McCafferty, keeping his head down, making the perfect rugby tackle: waist high, both arms open wide, then clamping around McCafferty's lower abdomen; the momentum and force of the tackle driving him backwards, downwards until he hit the wall. McCafferty's head whipped backwards and cracked against the wall so hard that he blacked out instantly and slipped lifelessly to the floor.

Peter, who was a bit dazed from the blow to his head, sat down next to McCafferty and gave himself a minute to recover before opening his backpack and removing the roll of duct tape. He used his knife to cut off a small strip of the tape and covered the wound on his head. He stood up and looked at himself in McCafferty's hall mirror. He looked a sight. However, now that he had stopped the bleeding, his attention turned to securing McCafferty before he came around.

Peter abandoned his original plan to torture McCafferty. He just wanted to get it over with and get out of there as quickly as possible. He tied McCafferty's hands behind his back with rope and covered his mouth and nose with duct tape. Within seconds, McCafferty's body began to wriggle and writhe—trying desperately to take in oxygen but failing. Suddenly, McCafferty's eyes opened wide in shock, staring at Peter, trying to comprehend why this was happening to him. He stopped moving after a couple of minutes, his body now limp. Peter checked for a pulse on his neck. *Nothing*. He then removed the tape and checked if he was breathing. Again, nothing. He quickly checked McCafferty's clothing and spotted some blood stains—his blood! He knew he would need to remove the blood-stained clothing and clean up any blood on the floor. Thankfully, it was smooth hardwood and not a carpet.

He went into the kitchen to find some floor cleaner and immediately could smell the spaghetti bolognaise in the oven. He turned it off, looked around the room and found a set of oven gloves. He removed the hot metal tray from the oven and placed it in the metal bin beside the back door. He then looked under the sink and found what he needed to clean the floor. He picked out a couple of cloths and headed to the hall, where he wiped up all the blood and then cleaned the area thoroughly with a bleach-based cleaner. He remembered Claire telling him that bleach could be used to destroy DNA, so with any luck, even if the police did find traces of his blood, it would not be able to be used to identify him. Satisfied that he had removed all the bloodstains from the floor, he moved onto McCafferty's clothing and started to strip him down, removing all of his external clothing. He took the clothes into the kitchen and found a bin liner under the sink. As he stood up, he noticed a door at the back of the kitchen. *What's through there?* He opened the door and could see that it led to the garage. Sitting in the middle of the tight garage space was a white Mercedes Benz, and that's when it came to Peter. He knew what he had to do.

Chapter 53

Claire and Carter were sitting in the incident room feeling incredibly pleased with themselves. Carter had called the whole team together to thank them for their excellent work and to brief them on the final outcome of the case.

"So, according to Maclean, he planned the whole thing himself. He had watched the Donaldson's house on several occasions before exacting his revenge and quickly realised that Mrs Donaldson nearly always went to bed first, while her husband worked late in his study and helped himself to a nightcap or two. On the night of the murder, he waited until Mrs Donaldson's bedroom light went out and then went to the front door and knocked just loud enough to be heard by Michael Donaldson, who promptly answered the door and invited Maclean into his study."

"Why did he invite him in at that time of night?" asked Doyle. "Seems a bit odd."

"Good question. Maclean claims that he pretended to need Donaldson's advice and support on a planning application to expand his property and gardening business. Donaldson, always keen to help one of his constituents, bought the lie and invited Maclean inside to discuss his proposal. During the conversation, Donaldson stood up and offered Maclean a whisky as he was going to have one himself. Maclean was counting on this. Donaldson poured two healthy measures and handed one to Maclean, who took a large gulp, pretended to cough as if he was choking and asked for some water. While Donaldson fetched the water from the kitchen, Maclean poured a small bottle of his homemade poison 'viscumin' into Donaldson's glass and continued coughing until Donaldson returned."

"Viscumin?" asked Doyle.

"Yes, pretty unusual I know, but apparently can be extracted from mistletoe if you know what you are doing," Carter explained.

"And Maclean had a chemistry set in his greenhouse," said Paul.

"Exactly," said Carter. "Anyway, Maclean sipped the water, poured some into his whisky to weaken it, then continued talking. At some point, Michael finished off his nightcap and then started to feel unwell. He asked Maclean to call an ambulance as he was now struggling to breathe. He thought he was having a heart attack, which he was - that's what viscumin does, it attacks the heart. Maclean pretended to make the call and told Donaldson that it would take an hour for the ambulance to get there. He then offered to take Michael to the hospital in his car."

"So that's how he managed to get him out of the house without any fuss or mess," said Claire.

"Yes, he walked Donaldson right out of the front door and put him in the backseat of his jeep, where he died. Maclean then returned to the study, put on a pair of gloves and quickly wiped down any surfaces he had touched. He then took both used whisky glasses into the kitchen, washed and dried them, and returned them to the study."

"Bloody genius!" offered Doyle.

"Indeed," said Carter.

"The rest, which he confirmed, we had pretty much worked out from the evidence. The use of the tractor to get Donaldson all the way to the tree and then to haul up his dead weight."

"Not to mention the use of the tree and the coins as the biggest red herring I've ever seen," said Claire.

Carter nodded. "Yeah, that too. All to lead us off in the wrong direction. And you know, if it hadn't been for that piece of glass embedded in the tractor tyre, he probably would have gotten away with murder."

The room fell silent as they all contemplated that particularly unnerving outcome.

"Right, so we still have a lot of paperwork to do, but that can wait until tomorrow. Who's all coming to the pub? Drinks are on me!" shouted Carter.

There were shouts and cheers as the team celebrated their success. Claire went over to Carter. "Which pub? I'll join you after I've been to see Brian."

"Probably the Abbotsford. We might need some food to soak up the beer! Oh, by the way, I heard the fraud team are now willing to investigate Donaldson's dealings with Munro and McLeish, so who knows, maybe we'll get a bit of credit for that bust too, if it goes down. Good work all round!"

"That's good to hear. Right, I'm off. I'll see you later."

Claire said her farewells to the rest of the team and made her way down to her car. A huge weight had been lifted from her shoulders and she felt good. Her only concern now was Brian and she prayed that he was still doing okay. They had become good friends over the past few years and she didn't know what she would do if anything happened to him. He was one of the reasons she hadn't agreed to join the organised crime team in Glasgow, but if he wasn't fit enough to return to duty, then perhaps she would reconsider. Carter had also mentioned the possibility of joining MIT; she had to admit that she had enjoyed working with him again. With that thought in mind, she started her car and headed to the Queen Elizabeth.

Chapter 54

Peter dragged McCafferty into the garage, which was much more difficult than he had first envisioned. He opened the car door and had to straddle McCafferty to lift his upper body into the front driver's seat as far as he could without falling over. He then went around to the passenger side and squeezed into the small gap between the wall and door, cursing whoever had designed such a ridiculously tight garage space. Once inside, he pulled McCafferty up onto the front seat and then twisted him into a seated position, leaving the dead man's legs hanging out of the driver's door. Peter then squeezed himself out of the passenger door, went back around the front of the car and lifted McCafferty's feet into the foot well. By the time he had finished all that manoeuvring, he was exhausted.

He took a moment to gather his thoughts and then found the garden hose at the other end of the garage, near the door. He removed the nozzle on the end of the hose, wiped it, and threw it aside. He then measured approximately ten feet of hose pipe and cut it with his knife. He took one end of the pipe and pushed it into the car exhaust and then, using his duct tape, sealed the end of the hose and the exhaust pipe. He then took the other end of the pipe to the front of the car. He switched on the ignition of the car and immediately smoke started to come out of the hose. *So far so good!*

He opened the driver-side window of the car just wide enough to squeeze in the hose and then closed the door. The cabin quickly filled with smoke. *Good!* Another thought suddenly came to him, and he opened the door and pulled more of the pipe through the gap in the window. Peter lifted McCafferty's head and put the hose pipe directly into McCafferty's mouth, then held his nose closed, ensuring the exhaust fumes made it all the way into McCafferty's lungs. Peter waited a full minute before removing the pipe and then closed the car door. He looked around and found the duct tape. He cleaned the outside of the tape and opened the door of the car again. He carefully pressed the tape against

McCafferty's right hand, ensuring he had left a good set of prints on the roll of the tape. He then wiped down his knife, placed it in McCafferty's hand to obtain prints, and then threw the knife and tape to the front of the garage. Finally, he wiped down the car doors, looked in the garage to make sure he hadn't missed anything and closed the garage door using the cloth.

There was a bag of McCafferty's blood-stained clothes and some stained cloths in a black bag lying in the hallway. Earlier, Peter had stripped McCafferty and dressed him with other clothes that he had found upstairs.

He went into the kitchen and wiped down everything he had touched, put on his backpack and then went back out to the hall and picked up the bin bag. He opened the front door slowly and looked down the street to see if anyone was coming. A set of headlights appeared at the entrance of the road, and Peter quickly pulled back inside and closed the door until the lights passed the house. He took another look, saw it was all clear and then casually walked away from the house and towards his car—his heart was racing and his head was throbbing. He reached his car safely and exhaled slowly. He had never been so scared in his life. He made up his mind there and then that it was over. He would return home and get on with his life. No more vendettas. He had gotten his revenge and would now focus on rebuilding his life with Claire, who thankfully was also showing signs of returning to her old self. He checked his phone and could see that Claire had been in touch. She had been to see Brian, who was remarkably chipper given his condition, and was now heading back to Dumbarton when she would drop into the Abbotsford as the team were there celebrating their success. She said to go ahead and eat, as she would probably be having something at the hotel. He smiled to himself. *Good. I'll have time to get in and get cleaned up.*

Chapter 55

Claire woke up feeling a bit groggy. She had met up with the team at the Abbotsford Hotel and had stayed until after 11.00 p.m. And, although she did have something to eat there, she wasn't used to drinking at the same pace as the others. She wondered what their heads were feeling like—after all, they had a good couple of hours extra drinking time. Carter, on the other hand, seemed to be unaffected by alcohol. Just as well, he wanted to be in court in the morning to hear Maclean's plea.

Claire made her way slowly downstairs and could smell the glorious aroma of eggs and bacon. "What's the occasion?" she asked.

Peter turned and smiled. "Good morning, did you have a good night then?"

"Yeah, it was good, but what on earth have you done to yourself?" she said, pointing to the large Elastoplast on his forehead.

"Oh that, it's just a scratch," he said, turning back to the frying pan, deliberately avoiding eye contact. "I took Sally for a walk in East End Park last night and let her off the lead thinking she would be safe. However, she caught sight of a rabbit in the trees and chased it all the way onto the railway line—there was a gap under the fence. Anyway, to cut a long story short, I scratched my head going under the fence."

Claire looked at Sally who, for no good reason at all, looked guilty. "You naughty girl, Sally! Chasing poor little rabbits and onto..." Claire was interrupted by the sound of the doorbell. "I'll get it," she said and headed for the door.

Claire tightened the belt on her nightgown to keep it closed over and then opened the door. To her surprise, she was met by two faces that she recognised. Standing there, looking equally surprised and a little confused, were DS Bell and DC McWilliams from Glasgow CID.

"DI Redding? Sorry, there must be some sort of mistake, we're looking for Peter Macdonald," said DC McWilliams.

Claire looked worried. "There's no mistake. He's here. We're married—what's this about? Has Peter done something wrong?"

"Sorry, but we need to speak to him in private," said DS Bell.

Claire knew what that meant. She turned and shouted into the kitchen, "Peter!" She waited until he appeared in the hallway. "There's two police officers here to see you."

Peter's face turned grey.

Claire stared at him, eyes beginning to water. "Peter, what have you done?"

The End.

About this book

All characters referred to within this book are fictitious and therefore any similarity to real people is coincidental. All views expressed within the book are fictitious in keeping with the storyline and are not the views of the author or the publisher.

Some of the buildings and places described within the story such as the Municipal Buildings and the Police HQ in Dumbarton are real in order give a feeling of reality to those who recognise them.

Books by Andrew Hawthorne

There's no such thing as a perfect crime

The Keeper

A Mug's Game

The End of the Line

For Children

Who put that Spaceship on my school?!

Printed in Great Britain
by Amazon